MIRRORED MINDS

A Novel by
Terri Lee

Library of congress number 2009910728
ISBN number 978-0-615-32621-4

Artwork designed by Zhanna Albertini.
Photography by Terpstra Photo
Book design by Karl Rouwhorst.

Printed in the United States of America by Color House Graphics, Incorporated, Grand Rapids, Michigan
10 9 8 7 6 5 4 3 2 1

To Rhonda and Bryan,

who make me proud everyday

Job 33:15-16

At night when people are asleep, God

speaks in dreams and visions.

PROLOGUE

Dreams can be a pathway into the inner sanctum of our minds, a method affording us to explore our spiritual self without interference from our physical presence – a journey toward another life awaiting its birth.

Why dreams occur and what they mean has been studied by many. There are numerous references in books and verses of the Bible that lend us to believe that interpreting dreams may work for good in life and family. Ancient Chinese tradition supports the belief that a person's spiritual soul creates our dreams allowing the body to travel to other realms and meet other souls.

The book of Corinthians I – 12:8-10 states: *The Spirit gives one person the power to work miracles; to another…. the ability to tell the difference between gifts that come from the Spirit and those that do not. To one person he gives the ability to speak in strange tongues, and to another he gives the ability to explain what is said, and in;*

Numbers 12:5-6 … and the Lord said, *"Now hear what I have to say! When there are prophets among you, I reveal myself to them in visions and speak to them in dreams."*

Edgar Cayce is one of America's famous psychics, often referred to as "the sleeping prophet". His ability to interpret people's dreams often astounded them. It was Cayce's belief that through dreaming, we had special access to our spiritual world.

The Edgar Cayce readings indicate that a dream can be of a physical, mental, or spiritual nature as well as tackling psychic manifestations such as; communication with beings in other realms, angels, telepathy or out of body traveling. Subconscious minds allow contact with one another giving us the chance to assist others in various ways, perhaps by bringing us helpful information or by seeking our aid through prayer.

Dreams come to you for a reason. Some elements of evolving dreams may reflect what comes to pass in the physical world or inwardly on some larger plane. What we choose to receive depends upon our level of acceptance.

Rudolf Steiner, the founder of Waldorf education has given us these thoughts to reflect upon – "A dream … is mostly connected with ideas (someone) had already acquired in his life, with reminiscences. These are however only the garments of what really lives in the dream or during sleep … for in dreams is revealed what actually takes place in the soul during sleep … (and the dream) is (also) related to the future … the soul is a prophet during our sleep…while we are asleep we do have to concern ourselves with the future."

The Skeptic's Dictionary-Robert Todd Carroll

THE WRITER

During the course of my life, I've become a believer in fate. Freewill has certainly played a part in the paths I've trodden and I sometimes reflect on what may have occurred had I chosen differently. I get curious about others whose lives have intersected mine at certain periods, wondering to the point of sheer exhaustion whether or not I should have acted upon our meeting, and where I could have gone or what I would have become if I had done so. I call these my fantasy episodes, for how could we speculate realistically on what might have been? After all, these musings always have a better outcome than the ones we are actually living, more adventurous and certainly more prosperous. It does no good to go on in such a way though as it only results in making me feel lacking, less successful.

On days when the weather is right – the temperature mild, mid-seventies or thereabout, I have lunch in the park. Maybe a slight breeze crosses my face cooling me off just at the point I begin to feel too warm, drying the small beads of sweat that had begun to form above my lips. If you've ever lived on the East Coast, you understand the kind of day I mean. These days don't occur nearly often enough. Eating lunch is secondary. The main enjoyment centers on others out enjoying the day also. I usually sit at the edge of a circled area of benches, affording me a clear view of the surroundings, then settle in to observe. My gaze latches on to a random soul or sometimes a family or group of teens. I release my mind allowing it to wander freely. Before long, I begin to wonder what their lives are like, if they are following their dreams or if circumstances have put them in a place they'd like to escape.

As in all communities these days, there are people wandering the streets, homeless. A few gather together talking underneath the shade of the trees, their bags or shopping carts parked nearby filled with items considered essential to their existence; others walk alone – an old man dressed in salvaged clothes too big for his slight frame, digging through garbage receptacles for pop cans either discarded purposefully for that reason or because the time required to return it was too precious to waste – a young woman leaning heavily on a walker, body tilted to one side her legs twisted at such an angle she walks on the insides of her feet. She talks out loud though no one is listening. I begin to conjure images of possible situations about whom or what was responsible for bringing them to this point. I contemplate what hidden history exists behind those vacant eyes, trying further to imagine what they're thinking at this very moment – if their thoughts are centered on finding a comfortable place to sleep tonight or on memories of finer times long gone. Perhaps they dream of the future hoping a better one is coming their way or possibly they've given up – become disillusioned at what life has offered them or taken away.

Day after day the media touts people stories. Around the clock captivating stories with horrific details or tales of feats so wondrous we ponder our own self-worth. Newspapers, magazines, television reality shows and talk shows on and on they go. The tag lines used are often misleading, merely crafted to draw our attention, urging us to read on. Eventually, we learn we've been manipulated with the real story buried beneath all the hoopla – yet the damage cannot be undone to the poor souls they've exploited to boost their ratings.

This leads me to thoughts of people considered average. People like me and perhaps you, living life each day outside of the limelight – never known by many but whose lives are sincere and selfless, their stories never having been told but important and at times life changing.

A while back, I was on vacation on the west coast. I'd been on a sightseeing adventure most of the morning and decided to rest on a bench nearby. It was a cool fall day but the sun shone bright across my face and I was soaking it in. I could feel its warmth course through me, while I followed the flow of ripples in the water of a small creek nearby. I must have been lost in thought for a moment or perhaps a non-thought, because I don't recall thinking of anything really. Anyway, I caught sight of movement to my left, prompting me to look up. On a bench next to me there was a young man – a hippy sort, lying prone on his stomach, arms crossed over each other, his chin resting on his hands – watching me. A worn backpack was sitting alongside him suggesting he was in transit from somewhere, maybe wandering across the country to find himself, I thought. When our eyes locked, he simply smiled a slight smile but with a hint of playfulness in it. I got the feeling he was granting me permission to share his space and the view, as if it belonged to him alone. I felt strangely guilty, so I smiled back as a gesture in acknowledging his gift. Suddenly, he jumped up leaving his pack where it lay and scurried away. I found myself looking after him, wondering if he had been a messenger sent to enlighten me.

The scenarios we imagine can take us anywhere we like, leaving us inspired or puzzled, the choice is left to our moods or creativity at any given time or place. I believe as many others do, that people are placed on this earth for a purpose and none of us are any less or any better than the other. Everyone contributes something to someone or to some place in this life. While we don't always understand what it is we're here for, we need to believe in our significance, our importance, the gifts we all have to share and the differences we can make. All of us have a story to tell. We just need someone to hear it. The question is whether anyone will take time to listen.

I have been a good person most of my life. I tried to follow the rules of society and those taught me by my parents. I attempted to pass down these basic principles, with a few deletions or additions for improvement, on to my own children.

I have also been a liar, most often to conceal my wrong doings and to protect others from the truth when the rawness of evil rises with distaste in my mouth. For inside of me, there exists a secret self I keep tucked beneath the surface, which in my younger years nearly caused my self destruction. I have grown in many ways since, in a movement toward goodness, pushing this hidden stranger into a smaller space inside me. It is this dark spot that invades my thoughts making me question my abilities, always feeding my doubts, repeatedly reminding me of my faults, my past mistakes. It is the inherent struggle of good and evil that lives within us all.

My struggle continues even now. I've lost direction, unsure of where I'm headed. I can find no reason for feeling this way. In many ways, I've been blessed. My family cares for me, yet I feel disconnected somehow. My children are grown with lives of their own and doing quite well, by middle class standards. My spouse is a gentle person, still in love with me in spite of myself. I question why I feel such a void, this emptiness threatening to devour me.

I am a master at hiding my inner feelings, always careful to mask my discontent, fearful it would disappoint them, as if they had failed me somehow. I've felt life should be led to its fullest, so a great deal of my sadness comes from a lack of satisfaction with my job. My duties require little effort to perform, yet I need to continue to stay like many others do – to pay the bills and build a nest egg for those golden years just around the corner.

I know I am not alone. These others I watch must face this challenge as I do, some less, some more. The balances vary – a result of life's placement in society or situations encountered along the way, thus – cause and effect. We are born with gifts. Some have voices with which they sing, some the ability to teach our children and others the skills needed to save lives. I am a lover of words, only after all this time, I still don't know how or what I can give with mere words. I search my soul looking for a glimmer of hope, an opportunity to do something that gives my life purpose. I begin by delving into my faith – by asking for guidance through prayers whispered at night while I lay in my bed. I seek to make a difference. I aim to leave a mark.

I awoke with a start at precisely 3:04 a.m. Friday on a sunny fall morning, September 23, 2005. I remember vividly every detail, a prayer was answered and my life began to take on a new direction with me a spectator along for the ride.

I rushed downstairs and began to write.

Jeremiah 29:11

"For I know the plans I have for you" declares the Lord,

"plans to prosper you and not to harm you, plans to give you

hope and a future."

THE STORY

THE EMERGENCY ROOM –
June 1981

Maryland

The scene is one of silence. The workers stand ready to put their skills in play. The quietness is eerie yet a sense of anticipation fills the room. It is not something unfamiliar to them. Similar scenarios are carried out over and over in hospitals across the country. It is what takes place in the Emergency Room. It is what medical personnel, like me, sign on to do when they choose the medical field. It takes a special person to work with people sick or injured. You have to possess certain strengths of character in order to separate your personal life from those you treat daily whose illnesses and suffering are painful to watch. This can be difficult in all areas of the medical profession, but when you're part of a trauma team, it can be even more conflicting.

This particular emergency involves a family of five. The Emergency Medical Technicians or EMTs have called ahead to assist the hospital in its preparation for the arrival of the injured, also providing a quick assessment of their conditions. From what I've been able to glean thus far, it isn't good. Two victims have not survived, although the official declaration of death will be conducted by a physician upon arrival.

Ours is not the closest hospital on the coast but the only one prepared to handle trauma cases of such magnitude, thus the decision was made to travel the extra miles needed, to gain the best chance of survival.

Everyone tenses upon hearing the sirens in the distance. It won't be long now and our hearts beat faster. The doctors and nurses double check the supplies – a perfunctory practice performed mostly as a means to keep focused. The lead ER physician assures himself the rooms are ready while issuing a few final preparatory instructions to his teams.

Suddenly, the doors burst open and the flurry of activity to save lives is underway. I stand back to allow the stretchers through offering assistance by pointing the way to the various rooms set up and waiting. My job requires me to standby for the moment, for I am the psychologist. My skills will be called upon at a later time when those that survive are in need of a seasoned veteran of calamity, who can assist them in dealing with the aftermath. Most survivors reach out for a person to help them make sense of what happened, to provide reassurance and support them in their grief. Anyone, who can offer answers, if possible, to "The Why's". Those that don't will require extra care to keep them from collapsing or becoming suicidal. It is I who will become their sounding board. I will take the brunt of their discontent. I will listen and hear of the ones who can no longer speak.

As the carts wheel by, I watch them one by one, two young boys appearing to be in their teens, a young girl with the face of an angel merely resting despite the matted blood in her long blond tresses. Next to enter is the Mother, clearly in distress, mumbling incoherently. Lastly, they wheel in the father, who emits a strong presence though silent. They are rushed to the rooms, engulfed by the doctors and nurses as the fight for life efforts begin. The largest room contains the boys with the mother alongside, only a curtain separating them. The direction of placement is expertly routed by the lead physician based upon his skilled assessment of the injuries. Father and daughter are wheeled to a separate room as they were the two casualties at the scene, their official declaration of death thus pronounced upon arrival.

While I wait to see where I am needed, I drift to the room where the father and daughter lie and begin to ponder all they will miss. The girl appears so fragile, a delicate cup of china unique in design – a creation like no other in the world. She is reminiscent of a storybook princess with blond hair spun from gold. Her skin is porcelain. She lies in wait for the kiss from her prince that will awaken her only her perfect lips will never feel its soft touch. Her slender finger will never have a wedding ring gently slipped on by the man of her dreams, nor will her hands caress the face of her newborn child or lift a rose to catch its sweet smell.

I glance over to her father knowing he too will never experience the joy of grandchildren. There will be no chance to pass along his history or teach them to sing songs or hook a fish.

Together, they will never walk down the aisle of a church, she in her wedding gown he in his tux. I wonder if they ever danced or shared the closeness many Dads and daughters do. Will they be together in the afterlife? Will they know what's been lost and long for life? Will they grieve as we grieve on earth? These are questions that remain a mystery to us all.

I return to the area where the team works fervently to save the boys and the mother. Ultimately, both the boys succumb to their injuries falling prey to the call of death, while their Mother, still embroiled in her own battle of survival, lies next to them unknowing.

The EMTs, who have stayed around waiting to hear of the outcomes, are discussing what they know of the accident. They describe how mangled the car was. So much so, they were required to use the jaws-of-life to free the victims. They voice their disbelief that anyone at all could live. The pavement was slick from a heavy rain causing the car to hydroplane at the unfortunate instant it was passing a semi. The entire right side of the vehicle was pushed into the back, only the left driver's side remaining partially intact. The father and daughter were seated on the right, the boys next to their sister in back. All suffered severe head trauma.

The only likely survivor will be the mother, who aside from the injuries to her skull, appears to have broken her shoulder blade causing significant pain with each breath. They are working to stabilize her now. She has a large bump on her head that is initiating a build up of fluid in her brain, the most urgent injury eliciting attention. Surgery is being arranged to reduce the pressure.

I ask the Doctors for time to enter her room while they wait for the surgical team to gather and they agree to a couple of minutes. I want to tell her I'll be here for her, let her hear the sound of my voice reassuring her – help her maintain the will to live. Since she was in and out of consciousness it's hard to know if she's aware of her family's injuries or whether or not she was alert enough to feel the blanket of death surrounding them. She may already be attempting to block any images to avoid the truth.

Entering her room I am struck by the number of tubes protruding from various locations on her body, the machinery surrounding her, the bandages already placed across the open wounds inflicted by the car's metal. There is only a portion of her face exposed appearing strangely untouched – a small perfect area in the shape of a three quarter moon, one you might gaze at on a clear summer's night. I hesitate briefly gathering my thoughts before I lean in close to whisper a message of hope in her ear.

Walking out of the room, I see a few nurses silently weeping, exhausted from the frantic activity only to have lost all but one. Other team members locate spots nearby pausing to reflect, thinking of their own families and the swiftness by which life changes.

The emergency room falls silent once again.

TOM – THE PSYCHOLOGIST

I met Maddy under tragic circumstances. That day – in the Emergency Room – was the first time in my career I lost focus. Medical personnel are trained to be stoic, hold their feelings in check, and not let "it" or "them" get to you and never on a personal level, at least one you can't break free of. The lives of those we treat are not supposed to crack our protective shell.

As a psychologist, it's my job to help people emotionally heal. It is what I've always wanted to do, for as long as I can remember. I believe this desire to be a direct result of growing up in an environment quite the opposite. My parents were self-centered types, except toward each other. They were a team, co-conspirators. Unfortunately, my brother and I were an intrusion. I'm sure they cared about us; at least I like to think they did, but they weren't adept at conveying those feelings on any consistent basis. Their form of loving existed when you did as you were told, didn't cause trouble or give them a reason to be displeased with you. Knowing exactly what it was you could do, to keep them happy or not, was a challenge my brother and I faced day-to-day. Many times we failed in this discovery and ultimately suffered the consequences. Mind you, we were never, or

I should say rarely, laid a hand on, but the verbal lashings were just as damaging, causing us to wish for a quick slap. There was no such thing as a discussion taking place during these informative sessions, for its definition would imply a conversation transpired between the parties involved. In our case, only one person would be vocalizing his wishes — my father. We were not permitted to talk or dare question why we were being punished. We rarely knew what action or inaction had crossed the line. His lectures focused on our badness without courtesy of an explanation. As a result, whatever we had done was apt to occur again through simple lack of knowledge.

The good side of this is: I became interested in listening to what people felt. Through this development of attentive listening methods, I also learned to read a client's body language, which often tells more than spoken words. As might be expected, my first client was my younger brother, who had a harder time understanding how to be good. He was forever being chastised by my parents, constantly raising their ire. I became his sole refuge for release. My listening helped relieve my brother's anger while I honed my skills for future use. I like to think the advice I offered him then, helped shape my brother into the caring husband and father he is today. His state of mind is alarmingly balanced. His longing to prove them wrong provided the motivation he needed to persevere, leading him to a successful career as an elementary school teacher.

I've always managed to maintain a level head, never allowing emotions to encumber professional doctrine. This balance can be tricky, but I believe it is the best way to service clients. Getting too emotional can interfere with objectivity. Sentiments can lead to failure by clouding your judgment. Not everyone can separate themselves from the feelings that sometimes swim just below the surface and though not every client can stir up these sensations, the ones that do – require control. This imposed restraint often crosses over to your personal life, stunting ones ability to let go of their senses. This has been the case for me. Hence, I am a forty-two year old, devoutly single male. I enjoy my brother and his family on the few days I take off to relax, which has usually fulfilled any shortcomings I have experienced at times – until the accident.

I think I knew the moment I saw her, my life was about to change. The skills I'd perfected would be challenged further than I thought possible. On this day, I dropped my armor letting Madelyn penetrate my soul unencumbered. How my life would be affected was uncertain. She was oblivious to the world around her, totally unaware of our connection or how her life had been altered – forever.

THE PARENTS

"Could you help us please?"

The Emergency Room desk clerk looks up at an elderly couple frantic, eyes pleading. The woman, bordering on panic, was clinging to her husband's arm. The clerk perceives them to be relatives of the family brought in earlier and she immediately stands up to offer assistance and usher them to a private room. Attempting to calm them as they walk, her suspicion of their connection is soon confirmed.

"Can you tell us how they are? Do you know what's happened to our daughter, our grandchildren? Have they been hurt badly? Can we see them?" The woman spews the questions rapidly, hardly a breath taken in between. The man tries to quiet her, though he too is clearly shaken.

"Please, wait here. I'll get the Doctor right away to talk with you. He'll be here quickly, I'm sure of it." The desk clerk scurries away through the Emergency Room doors to search for the Doctor. Her heart is heavy and filled with sorrow for the two people she leaves waiting. The news of the heartbreaking situation that has unfolded during the past few hours has spread throughout the hospital. These types of cases are the ones that cause her anxiety and elicit concern for her own family, while at the same time bring forth an appreciation for them too, because for now – they are safe. She catches sight of the Emergency Room doctor as he is headed back to the room where the Mother fights for her life.

"Doctor Starr, an elderly couple has just arrived – relatives of the accident victims. I've put them in a private room. They are extremely distraught as you can imagine. Can you speak with them please? They've driven a long way without knowing what has happened. I'm not certain they can wait much longer."

His face clouds over and his eyes show the sadness he feels in his heart. He nods his head turning to follow the clerk out. This is the hardest part of his job. This isn't a simple illness he can fix or one he can control. This is death, this is real, and this sucks! And you never get used to it. In medical school there are lectures on proven approach methods, the correct ways to deliver poor test results altering prolonged health, discussions of terminal illness or death, but nothing can ready a person for the actual event. You draw on your reserves, doing the best you can to soften the blow. He begins gathering the positives in his head, the fact their daughter is still clinging to life, currently stable. She is still critical and will be prepared for surgery soon to reduce the swelling in her brain, but he wants to give them something to cling to, some semblance of hope amid the chaos. God knows they will need it. Then, as he opens the door seeing their faces, he wonders if there is a God.

They look up immediately as he walks into the room. Before they can stand, he crosses the room with long strides and extends his hand out toward them, gently touching the man's shoulder as he pulls a nearby chair over to face them.

"I'm Dr. Starr and you are?"

"My name is Paul Weber and this is my wife, Rose." "We're Madelyn's parents, Madelyn Grayson. Please tell us how they are? The police only told us there was an accident and we should get here right away."

"Your daughter is alive Mr. and Mrs. Weber. The staff is stabilizing her now. She has suffered a great deal of head trauma, which has caused some swelling. We are preparing her for surgery to avoid further pressure on her brain. She has periods of lucidity but we're trying to keep her calm. We're awaiting the results of X-rays, but believe she has also broken her shoulder blade which is causing her some breathing difficulty and pain. We are taking every precaution…"

He is interrupted by Mrs. Weber, "Can you tell us anything about our grandchildren and our son-in-law? Are they going to be all right? You haven't said a word about them."

"I'm afraid the news isn't good." He hesitates briefly, his mouth suddenly dry and while he struggles to form the right words, he can see the fluids forming in her eyes threatening to break free. In a soft voice he begins again. "I'm sorry – your granddaughter and son-in-law died instantly. We tried our best to save your grandsons but………"

As I turn to look at my husband, I no longer hear the Doctors words. Paul's face confirms the awful truth I've just heard. The numbness begins in my fingertips inching its way along until I no longer feel my hands, my mind begins drifting away, shutting down so I can block out the awful truth. I start to shake as a cold emptiness overtakes my body. Within seconds my legs give way and I fold into myself, like one of my granddaughter, Lucy's paper dolls she used to play with at the kitchen table. I smile inside at the thought momentarily then -there is nothing. When I awake, I am lying on the couch. Paul is holding my hand and the Doctor, what was his name? Anyway, he is checking my pulse. I peer up at them through a narrow tunnel while they stare at me from its other side as though studying an object through a microscope.

"Rose, oh Rose" says Paul with tears streaming down his face. He squeezes my hands trying his best to be strong. As the memory of the Doctor's words hit my mind once again, I softly begin to weep. Paul leans his head into mine and I feel his lips brushing over my forehead, gently whispering that it will be Okay, using all his might to convince me, except I know he doesn't believe it either. Nothing will ever be good again, not like before. Our grandchildren are gone, all of them, in the time it takes a glass to slip from a hand and shatter into a thousand pieces across the floor; along with our beloved son-in-law, Neil – the son we never had. My thoughts drift to my daughter and how she will cope. She will need her Mother. I begin to harness my nurturing instincts focusing my mind on Madelyn. Sitting up, I look directly at the doctor when I say,

"Dr. Starr, I think we need to see our daughter now."

"Of course, Mrs. Weber, only I should remind you she is barely conscious and not fully aware of what's happened, but yes, of course you can see her. Are you able to stand? I can get you a wheelchair if you like."

"No, no. I'll manage. You've been very kind. I wasn't expecting them all … well; it's such a shock…. I'll feel much better if I see her, and Dr., one more thing…" I glance over at Paul for acceptance. He nods his head in a positive response knowing me well enough to predict my next request.

"Could we see them too – just for a moment?"

Once again, my strength waivers as I attempt to stand, but I reach out for Paul's arm grasping it tightly. Steadying myself against him, he places his arm protectively around my shoulders until I can recover well enough to walk. I wonder how we will endure this next task. Hovering closely together, we move along the colorless corridor that leads us toward the unknown.

OBSERVATIONS

With my treatment plan in hand, I watch Madelyn's parents through the glass. The Webers have experienced a tremendous loss at a time in their lives they should be able to relax. It is never the norm for one to lose a child or grandchild. It doesn't follow the standard progression of life as we expect it to be, tilting its balance. Their current focus centers on their ability to hang on to the only loved one left – she laying silent, unable to share in their grief thus depriving them of their need to comfort her. Day after day, clinging to each other for strength, they wait, watching for signs of awareness. I've learned bits and pieces about Rose and Paul during my visits to their daughter and also in sessions I've held with them.

Rose comes from a prominent family of Boston, Massachusetts having grown-up among the elite. Paul grew up in a suburb close by studying dentistry at Boston University School of Dental Medicine setting up his own practice in Falls River. This is how he met Rose – an abscess of her upper molar. Impressed with her grace under such profound pain, he asked her for a date. They were married a year later. Madelyn is their only child. They call her Maddy.

Madelyn's condition is currently stable although she exists in a coma. The doctors were successful in reducing the swelling in her brain expecting her to enter this comatose condition for a period. They had hoped it would be temporary, perhaps a couple of weeks only it's continued beyond that, which is causing concern. The crucial issue is that it not last indefinitely, no longer than a month is what they consider safe. This timeframe is considered an acceptable period based on historical records to avoid prolonged damage to the brain allowing it to retain its full function.

Three weeks have passed now. Hope is beginning to wane. This tension is coupled with the Webers' past concern over her failure to recognize their faces or voices when they briefly visited her in the Emergency Room. Her comments uttered bore no recognition of a family connection – no signs of knowing who they were.

Besides her head trauma, Madelyn's body is covered with bruises in transition from varying shades of purple to yellow, as they enter the healing phase, the stitches from cuts are now gone yet the scarring left behind is still raised and reddened. Her broken shoulder blade is immobilized by a shoulder sling with ice packs to reduce swelling and pain medication to ease her discomfort. A physical therapist performs a series of exercises daily to improve her range of shoulder motion, since she lacks the ability to move on her own. Madelyn also sustained trauma to her spinal cord though she had movement in her legs upon her arrival, so her prospects for walking again are good. Whatever the end result, she is facing a considerable amount of time in rehabilitation. What isn't known is whether she possesses the desire to survive and this thought is what weighs heavily on her parent's minds. They are anxious for her to wake up though fearful she will for this is when they will have to tell her that her family is gone. This is when she will have to face facts. This is when they will have to tell her about the funeral, the four caskets sitting side-by-side in the church, an event she missed. Her last chance to see them, touch them, gone forever.

One of the hardest conversations I had with them involved the day of the funerals. It had been a couple of weeks after and I sensed they needed to talk about it with someone. They wanted to get their feelings out before it tore them apart inside, especially Rose. My office was a sanctuary for them, a place they could let go of their reserves and allow their emotions to be exposed, raw and unbridled. I remember the day well. Rose was fidgeting with her hanky, twisting it so tightly in her hands it began to form a knot. Paul just sat watching the action intrigued by the stress it absorbed.

"Rose, do you think it would help if you talked about the funeral? I know it will be hard, but maybe if you spoke aloud your thoughts, it could help you release some of the emotions you're trying so hard to suppress."

She glanced up at me for a moment and I waited while she considered my suggestion. I watched her take a deep breath then slowly release it. Apprehensive, but trusting my motives, she began to speak.

"I keep seeing them, even when my eyes are open, Tom. I see their faces, then the caskets – back and forth, over and over. Much of the day is a blur, except for that image. We decided ahead of time to keep the caskets closed. We felt they wouldn't want their close friends to see them in death. I couldn't decide where to look. I found my eyes moving among the three children's caskets, first one then the other, trying to make sure I spread my grief evenly. Isn't that crazy? When the children were little they would compete for my attention always wanting time with me. I was trying to be fair by sharing my grief for each of them equally. My head began to ache with the constant flitting around, so I looked down instead. I don't even remember what else happened, although some of their friends must have paid tribute. When the service ended, Paul and I went up to say our last goodbyes. I touched each of their caskets as I passed, lingering only long enough to send them off one final time as I always did on our visits. I love you, Neil. I love you, Ian. I love you, Jon. I love you, Lucy."

Only then did she breakdown, allowing her grief to spill out while Paul held her tightly and I did my best to comfort them both. Before they left that day, Rose thanked me for listening saying she felt relieved, at peace.

This couple has taken on so much, I worry they might crumble under the weight. Their strength thus far has amazed me. Their resolve is admirable. At times I think they are what sustain me, affording me the tenacity I need to perform effectively.

With doubts threatening to invade my mind, I take a deep breath, put on a smile and reach for the handle of the door.

ROSE

I awoke this morning to a bright sunny cloudless day. A vibrant stream of yellow juts through the bedroom curtains and lies neatly across my legs. For a brief period, I simply relish in the peacefulness of the moment thinking back on earlier times.

Being a Mother is such a demanding job. To be entrusted to mold a life from its very conception is a tremendous task God places in our hands. I've always felt I'd done a fair job at it even though I was only blessed with one opportunity to get it right. I suppose I made many mistakes along the way, but I figured I hadn't faired too badly as my daughter and I still shared a close bond with one another. Looking back, I wish I'd have spent more time with Madelyn as a child. I was always so busy with my society functions and volunteer activities, I'm afraid I pushed her too hard. Always expecting her to behave properly, stay clean, and mind her manners.

"You mustn't fidget dear", I would say to her. "You mustn't let people think you don't want to be here or you will offend them. Be pleasant, dear. Smile and say Hello, when they talk to you, but only if they speak first. Children should be seen, not heard, Madelyn."

She would always reply, "Yes, Momma. I'll be good."

I can still remember her sitting very still, afraid to move lest she ruffle her dress or scuff her shoes. She was the perfect child and my bridge club reveled in how well behaved she was. She never complained, even after she'd grown up.

After the grandchildren came along though, I saw how differently, Maddy raised them. Oh, they were polite all right, but she allowed them to be children, not porcelain dolls in a corner. I brought the subject up one time when Maddy and I met for lunch one day and of course, the ever dutiful daughter assured me I had been a wonderful Mother. "Times are different now", she'd say, but I knew I should have spent more time doing the little things, playing games and make believe. I did have a chance to be less stringent with my grandchildren, and for that I am grateful. They taught me how to relax, take time to hug and to laugh when things weren't perfect.

Reality surfaces once again and the darkness inside me forms into clouds so thick, even a sunny day can't penetrate the shadows threatening to envelope my soul. Thoughts of all that has transpired these past few weeks begin to enter my mind, tripping over each other until I scream aloud within, and pray for them to stop. Methodically, I pick them apart, mentally organizing them, one at a time so once more I can maintain order and make it through another day. The days of relaxation and enjoyment are gone now, forever. I return to the strictness of control and detachment, locking my feelings deep inside once more lest my exterior facade begin to crack.

On the day Paul and I arrived at the hospital, the day of the accident, I saw little hope. Seeing our son-in-law and grandchildren in utter silence, hauntingly still is an image I would like to erase from my brain. I knew I was viewing only their shells no longer vibrant with life, their souls having moved on to a place I could only wonder about. Oddly, I felt a presence – a type of comfort I cannot explain.

I was certain they knew of my grief and I could feel their sorrow fill the room at their inability to cross over and wrap me in their arms. The mere thought of the possibility brought warmth to my heart.

Afterward, we went to our daughter who was in a battle of her own. Although we wanted desperately for her to survive, we were also afraid she would, a conflict of emotions impossible to fathom. How would she cope with this cruel twist of fate when we could barely handle it? Her family had been her joy, her focus and she wore their many achievements like a medal of honor – for it was she who nurtured them. They were all so close, so caring, so giving.

The first week was touch and go for Madelyn, our thoughts and prayers consumed with her condition. We waited as long as we could to make funeral arrangements hoping every day Maddy would wake up. We wanted her to have her chance to say goodbye, to help us with decisions we could only guess at. Did they want a burial or cremation? These are things we never discussed, after all, weren't we the ones that should have gone on first? Shouldn't they be making funeral arrangements for us?

In the end, we made those decisions for her. We greeted the children's school friends and Maddy and Neil's friends also. We answered their questions doling out comfort to those close to them – some we knew and others we had never met. While Maddy lay oblivious to everything, barely hanging on. Ultimately, we decided to have them cremated in hopes Madelyn could one day find closure in the spreading of their ashes.

Since then, we've split our time between hospital visits with Maddy and sewing up the loose ends of their lives by pouring through paperwork, life insurance policies and other bills to sort out the things that take precedence when illness strikes. We also visited colleges & workplaces packing up mementos, pictures and other paraphernalia we all tend to collect. We are strong because we have to be. Besides, keeping a focus on details keeps our minds occupied on tasks, moving along like robots void of sentiment. We do it for our daughter, so she won't have to worry about such things when she wakes up.

I recall our first visit to their house in the days following the accident. I remember walking in with the feeling they were still there. I can't recollect a time when they weren't here waiting for us to arrive.

Opening the door with their key feels foreign to me, an unnatural act. I stifle the urge to call out. I force myself to refocus on the purpose of our visit and begin boxing away select pieces of their lives, small memories of a marriage and children to set aside in storage, awaiting Madelyn's return. I still hear echoes in the rooms, sounds off in the distance.

A child's record is playing in Lucy's room, a song she loved, as a little girl and a smile crosses my face as I recall her small voice singing;

You are my sunshine; my only sunshine, you make me happy when skies are gray, you'll never know dear how much I love you, please don't take my sunshine away.

Then, the sound of tiny footsteps – the twins running after each other — yet another game of cowboys and Indians I'd bet. Ian really wanted to be the cowboy but Jon always claimed first pick, since he was the oldest – by a couple of minutes. Jon was skilled in negotiating, a born leader. He could always convince Ian to see his plan as the best, while Ian ever the peacemaker was content to follow along. They were so sweet. Both would run up to me when I arrived, each clamoring for a spot inside my arms so I could give them their hugs.

The memory causes a tear to slide down my cheek flowing along a crease ending at the corner of my mouth. A hint of saltiness hits my tongue before my fingers wipe it away.

Again, I wrestle with the conflict inside me, wanting my daughter to awaken yet fearful she will. I miss her. Maybe today she will come back to us. Maybe today our daughter will talk. Maybe today we will have to tell her. Maybe today we will break her heart. There can be no completely safe or totally happy outcome. I cannot protect her. I can only stand by her – share her grief. We will talk of their goodness. We will remember their accomplishments. We will cherish the memories. We will learn to survive.

CHANGES

Paul and I arrive at the hospital shortly after lunch. The staff recognizes us as we enter nodding hello while we walk by. Lately, we have both been on edge. The critical one month deadline passed three days ago and our spirit is beginning to diminish. It's become harder to put forth a positive tone in our voices when talking to her. Before entering Madelyn's room, we take each others hand, silently praying for guidance then begin our routine.

"Hello Madelyn, its Mom and Dad dear", I say. We collectively lean in to plant a kiss on her forehead. We chatter about familiar things, things she will care about – friends, current events, her favorite television shows. Her eyes are open, but as usual, there is no recognition or association with the outside world. Does she see anything?

Paul sits down to read a book to her. I begin freshening the surroundings, opening the curtains to let in the sun and weeding out any flowers beginning to wilt in the plants and bouquets we've continually kept circulating on an in and out rotation. Her room is on the third floor facing east, providing the likelihood of catching a sunrise, a symbol of a new beginning. Her view is of a lush green landscape spotted with trees – Tulip Poplar with its majestic cone shape; the Aspako Grape, its bright red blooms rich with color and; the Weeping Willow whose graceful drooping branches fall like a canopy awaiting its chance to provide a shelter of comfort with its embrace. There's a walkway below weaving through a flower garden where patients can stroll or sit on benches to rest or reflect. Madelyn will like this. She always loved fresh flowers around her. It was common to see bouquets of flowers throughout her house, especially after she had cleaned. Her favorite was Freesia, its fragrance deliciously sweet. She loved the artistic look about them, the loose cluster of funnel-shaped flowers sitting atop the sharp bend of the stalk, always leaning to one side but facing upward toward the light. She would place small vases with a single stem in each bathroom – a natural perfume of beauty.

I walk into the lavatory to rinse out her water pitcher when I hear a slight murmur, causing me to stop abruptly and strain my ears to listen. Silence is the only thing I hear or can you even hear silence, I wonder. After all, if you don't hear anything, how can you say you're even hearing? You're rambling Rose, I think to myself – stay focused. I release my breath, not even aware I'd been holding it. I reach for the faucet when – there it is – another sound.

"Rose, get in here. She's stirring. Quick!"

Paul is standing next to the bed. I can barely feel my feet touching the linoleum, my heart beating so loudly I'm sure it can be heard down the hallway. As I reach Paul's side, she turns her head toward us. Her eyes strive to focus then settle briefly on mine in a plea to understand. She moves her mouth but only a raspy noise breaks forth – her movements become jerky, agitated.

"Don't try to talk Madelyn, stay calm."

"I'll get help", Paul says darting out of the room toward the nurse's station.

I know I should get her some water but I don't want to leave her, afraid she will fall back into herself again. Besides, she looks scared. I hope my presence gives her comfort. I stroke her arm gently "It's me Maddy. I'm here baby, I'm here." I continue talking gently coaxing her into staying with us while watching for signs she understands – a signal signifying her return.

REHABILITATION

In my head, I recite the information I've been told, making another attempt at comprehension. I figure if I repeat it often enough, something will finally penetrate the locked door of my memory.

"My name is Madelyn Grayson, Maddy for short. My parents are Rose and Paul Weber. I was born April 17, 1932. Recently, I turned 50. I grew up near Falls River south of Boston. I have an Interior Design Masters degree. I was married in 1957. My husband's name was Neil. He was a well known Architect. My daughter Lucy was born in 1959, my twin sons Ian and Jon were born three years later. We spent our summers at a Beach House we rented on the Outer Banks in North Carolina. We were happy. A devastating automobile accident occurred on, June 3, 1981. My entire family died, except me of course. I was lucky. I lived."

These are some facts I've been told. There are many others on my list. I remember nothing. Retrograde Amnesia is the term used to describe my condition I believe. This means I no longer remember events prior to my brain trauma, only those occurring post injuries. Rose and Paul (my parents) have been regular visitors, doing their best to prod my memory, along with my psychologist, Tom

Hammond and of course, my dearest of friends. I'm told their names are Mindy and Sarah. Everyone seems hopeful. I, on the other hand, am less positive, a little numb I suppose as in — I feel nothing at all. I can't relate to people, things or any situations from my past they describe. I want to, I truly do – but, I simply can't muster up the strength or the desire. I've had other distractions to work on these past months, like getting my right shoulder and arm to function properly again or move without exhausting all my energy within minutes. My legs feel limp like rubber bands stretched to a point where their elasticity has vanished.

I've been living at Collingswood Hills Rehabilitation Center since my transfer nine months ago, three months post crash. It's a top notch facility, I'm told.

I undergo physical therapy exercises to revive the muscles in my body no longer pliant. In addition, I undergo stimulation therapy, which works on my memory skills using the five senses – touch, sight, smell, taste and sound. My therapists say I'm a fighter. According to my parents, I always have been.

I was able to retain most of my basic knowledge. However, history was another matter. There is an expansive library here covering numerous topics. I receive audio books using earplugs so I can reconnect to past events as well as those current without disturbing my roommates. Another part of the healing process involves association with my peers, a Support Group. I'm not opposed to this type of treatment mind you, but most of the other patients here aren't dealing with the same type of situation I am. They've all suffered head trauma of some sort but most have some semblance of memory intact, a few holes here and there but they know who their family members are. They deal more in anger issues or frustrations resulting from their inability to focus. They wrestle with recapturing the "old self" getting glimpses from time to time. I, on the other hand, don't know who my "old self" is or was, hence not an issue of concern. I consider this a positive thing – no baggage. While I go along with the program as it's been laid out for me, I contribute only the minimum, electing to concentrate on what I might do now – looking to the future. After all, I've been born again right? Like a baby, inquisitive, learning as you go, opening up to the world around you.

I've been told I should be leaving here soon. Just a few more months and I'll be going home – to my parent's house, I think. This is strange to imagine at this age, but I no longer have a home of my own.

After the accident, there were many decisions to be made, which fell upon my parent's shoulders. They handled the burials of my husband and children while I languished in my comatose haze. They dealt with it all, which I imagine was extremely burdensome. Eventually, they were forced to sell my family's house, pack up our belongings and place them in storage. The money from this sale and from insurance policies was needed to supplement my rehabilitation costs. I know these things because they tell me, but without any connection to these material things I'm afraid I can't relate to their disposal. They determined what I may want unknowingly in the future. I'm grateful to them for taking charge of what must have been a difficult task to endure.

This whole thing is a little weird for me. I'm floating in limbo. It's like being handed a clean slate totally blank, waiting to be filled in. What would you do given such an opening? Would you be excited at the prospect to move forward or pulled down with the weight of the unknown? I chose the first. I am a survivor. This – is who I am now.

MASSACHUSETTS ROOTS

"Madelyn dear, is there anything I can help you with? The guests will be arriving soon. We mustn't keep them waiting. It wouldn't be proper."

"Of course not Mother, I'm almost ready.

My Mother has worked diligently to make this Christmas party a happy event. Since my arrival home in October, she and my father, have done all they can to make my transition into the outside world seamless and comfortable. At first they inundated me with information, recalling past events with family, friends and work associates, all in an attempt to trigger remembrance. These efforts failed repeatedly. Lately, they've stepped back, letting me approach them when I want help, giving me the space I need to recall on my own. Perhaps they've finally accepted my situation, a relief I can't describe.

Secretly, I'm certain my Mother holds out hope for full recovery. Experts agree the families are the most affected by an injured person's condition. It's been easier for me to face reality. I'm aware of what I can and cannot do any longer.

I've continued practicing the Memory Recall tasks they assigned me at Rehab, when I remember to do so. I much prefer the escape mechanisms I've developed on my own though. Imagining the past is significantly more fulfilling. The only real issue for me at this point is sleeping. Often times at night, I experience a recurring nightmare where I'm trapped in a confined space, unable to see what is around me. I cannot move at all nor can I speak. I see ghostlike images above me, but what or who they are is unclear. When I awake, I'm agitated for hours afterward.

My parents seem most resilient. They appear tireless in their efforts to meet my needs, which must be exhausting for them at their age. They deserve my respect, which I try to bestow upon them in my limited way. I wouldn't want to hurt them anymore as I know the accident and my resulting condition have certainly done enough damage. They have become my friends.

This party they've planned is another attempt at normalcy. It is a tradition they've followed for many years. I believe they've invited everyone they felt could provide mental stimulation potentially capable of tripping that final switch, bringing forth light into the darkened caverns of my mind. I was reintroduced to several of them through previous visits, some who've offered continued support despite my failure to reconnect. I am looking forward to a night filled with the scent of good food and conversation focused elsewhere instead of on me alone.

"Madelyn, our guests are arriving."

I move steadily along the corridor tabling my thoughts temporarily as I respond,

"Coming, Mom".

A FRIENDSHIP GROWS

After Rose and Paul leave my office, I look over their comments regarding Madelyn's progress. This past couple of years has been a long process for us all. I'm not sure who has shouldered the heaviest burden, the Webers, Madelyn or me. Each of us has faced uncertainty along our journey working hard on a solution.

Madelyn has put forth the most in physical effort often encountering painful movements without complaint. She's worked hard to strengthen the muscles in her shoulder to improve her range of motion and though her spinal bruising has healed nicely, her lower extremities tire easily so she pushes herself constantly, determined to grow stronger. When she's not exercising her body, she's exercising her mind. She absorbs everything.

In the beginning of our sessions, she seemed interested about the day of the accident, how it occurred and what I had heard. After a while though, it seemed too much for her to comprehend. I held some of the details regarding the accident back, such as; the fact she was driving. Her parents felt this knowledge might hinder her recovery and place too much of a burden on her so I agreed to withhold this information. I didn't lie. The specifics just never came up.

Besides, the crash couldn't have been avoided. The highway was slippery from the rain and the pool of water spread across the road caused the vehicle to hydroplane. Despite her inability to control the situation, her parents believed she would berate herself for causing her family's death, while she survived. Therefore, these details were left unspoken.

Eventually, she became agitated toward any subject relating to her personal past, interested mostly in historical matters or places of interest.

Her parents, Rose and Paul, have suffered the most emotionally. They've lost everything normal they once held precious. They are extremely happy to have their daughter, but she is no longer the person she once was. When a person can no longer remember their past they change, relationships change as well. At the start they held an abundance of faith this situation would correct itself someday and Madelyn would come back to them once again. Now, they're learning to love her in a different way and with different expectations for this altered life of hers. The pain of their loss is still fresh when they let it in, but they tell me this occurs less often now. They only want as we all do, what's best for Madelyn.

Then there is me. Madelyn has been my biggest challenge professionally. So much, I've begun to doubt my abilities as a therapist. I've spent countless hours in research looking for something, any kind of tool or method I may have overlooked or for any new experimental treatments that would break through the barriers blocking her return. Nothing has worked thus far but I continue to search unable to admit potential failure. My further mistake was in letting Madelyn penetrate my inner sanctum of feelings, the wall I had built around myself to keep patients at bay. This causes me to question my subjectivity. Of course, I've never let her know that and I never will.

She is much too fragile and she relies on me for my "outside" opinion. After all, I'm still a professional and I haven't forgotten my responsibilities to provide the best care for my patients. Hence, my silence on this subject is firm. Nonetheless, she invades my thoughts often in the night and I can't help but wonder what it would be like to be more than a friend for her, a confidant once removed. These thoughts always circle back to the beginning. She was a wife and Mother first. She deserves to know what that was like and it's my job to help her rediscover her past. This is exactly what I will do, if I'm able. One day, I may have to accept this recall may never happen. Should this conclusion be reached, I will also be responsible for getting her to accept that and encourage her to move on.

Soon, she will tire of the memory exercises and the struggle to remember. Soon, she will plead with me for a solution. Soon, I will have to face facts. Soon, I will have to let her go. Soon, she will leave to begin again.

LETTING GO

I believe a mother can sense her child's distress and lately I'm feeling some urgency in my daughter these days, a sullenness I cannot seem to penetrate. She has tried hard to regain a life her father and I keep telling her she had.

In the beginning, she patiently poured through old scrapbooks and other mementos we had saved from her childhood, her wedding photos and pictures of the children. I could see it in her eyes, at first the concentration of effort then, the light would dissipate and she had to stop. Nothing ever generated a spark. When I attempt to talk of past times now, she merely turns her head away drifting her focus elsewhere.

Her longtime friends, Sara and Mindy, tried to encircle her with their friendship once again, but it was difficult. She was no longer the Maddy they knew. She couldn't relate to past experiences and the outings they arranged for her weren't exactly met with enthusiasm. Maddy was different, quieter, more reserved and guarded, no longer the carefree fun-spirited girl they'd grown up with. She was the same in some ways, her strength and spirit of survival still present, but there was no longer a light or sparkle that shown in her eyes like before. Eventually, she no longer responded to their invites, so they dropped off all efforts to contact her.

We've tried stimulating her with shops we knew she used to love visiting and even the old company where she worked as a home design consultant. We drove by the home where she, Neil and the children used to live. All, I'm afraid, has been ineffective.

She's been such a good sport, but I feel her slipping away. I'm certain she's frustrated at her inability to please us. I know she can't remember us as her parents or the feeling that goes along with this bond, but I believe she cares for us and for that I'm grateful. She's as close as she can be right now. We've become friends in a way not all daughters and mothers can achieve.

Paul and I talked last night while we lie in bed and all was quiet. When I told him what I was feeling about Madelyn and how I felt her escalating sadness, he placed his arms around me and told me he has sensed it too. He had been waiting for me to recognize the signs, so I would be ready.

"Ready for what" I asked him.

"Ready to let her go" he whispered softly.

Tears began to fill my eyes and my chest grew heavy. I hadn't thought of what all this meant. I hadn't realized that in order to find herself she would have to leave us. I would lose her again. All parents have to let their children go. It's the natural order of things. God gives us our children to nurture, to instruct and to love, but our ultimate gift to them is to teach them how to live, how to survive in life and in the end letting them leave with our blessings. It's not that I hadn't done this before, but this time seemed much harder. We would be severing our relationship in a different way – that of friends more than parents and I worried we might never have a daughter again.

So this morning as I begin my morning regime, I steel myself for this next step I know I must take. I'm getting tired and the past couple of years have managed to chip away at my strength and poise. For Madelyn, I will draw all the reserve I have left to give my grown daughter what she needs, to help her move on in her journey – with sadness in my heart, a smile, and blessings on my lips.

LEAVING

It is early morning and my parents are still asleep. The buds on the trees outside are beginning to form. Each is at various stages of opening with some still bound tightly. Others are starting to separate, to form an array of bright petals that will eventually fill the limbs overflowing, causing some to bend slightly with their weight. They are the signs of springtime, my favorite time of year. The changes I observe are like watching an artist creating a painting. By squinting my eyes slightly I can change the contrast from distinct sharpness to blurred, altering its image to produce my own interpretation. I allow myself this small pleasure of merely watching, to enjoy the view as it unfolds – a distraction for what I know I must do.

My restlessness has been growing and at last I've come to a decision. It's time to leave here. I am growing weak in my ability to hide my true feelings and I can no longer use up energy in doing so. I've thought again about revisiting my old house and even traveling down to the beach in a last ditch attempt to recall the many summers we had spent there, but no matter – I would still not remember having been a part of it. The memory exercises have been futile and the steps I took along the way were simply that – only steps – no linking to the place in my mind where the memories sit dormant, no longer available for recall, simply gone. They are locked up tight, too deep to ever find again. This is why I must leave soon.

I communicated to Tom a few weeks back my growing frustrations. My eyes implored him to understand my needs, how I needed to stop this ritual of remembering and get on with my life. He took me by surprise by what he said. I've been thinking about it ever since.

"Look, Maddy" he said. "You know we've talked about the possibility you may never regain your past. I'm in support of whatever you feel you must do. You also know I want what is best for you, which is why I'm going to suggest something that may shock you. You need to move away, Maddy out of your parent's house, somewhere fresh and new. Go to a place where you can create your own life without reminders. Don't concern yourself with your parents. I'll talk to them. They've always put your needs first. They'll understand. You deserve a good life and I know your happiness is what matters to them. You need to stop beating yourself up with ghosts from the past and learn to forge ahead."

So here I am, trying to make sense of this life moving forward. I don't know why this has happened to me, these changes and what it all means, but I know Tom is right. I can't live in a past I don't know. I need to be me and I don't think I can figure out who I am here. The longer I stay the harder it will be to move on. I have a plan now.

I glance down at a paper in my hand. It's an ad about a small business opportunity in Landrum, South Carolina. A combination bookshop & coffee house for sale. Something drew my interest when I saw it and the wheels in my head began to turn. I began to imagine it taking shape. For the first time I could feel myself get excited about something again. I have a little money left from the sale of the house and I think this may be a good way to use it. It feels like the right thing to do. It will be a big challenge for me but a way to keep busy, meet new people and make new connections – things that won't always tug at me or pull at my heart strings. I won't have to see faces looking at me with pity for what I've been through or with anticipation that I may remember an event they describe. No one will know about my past. I'll be unsullied. The new Madelyn reincarnate. Instead of Maddy, I'll become Lyn. After all, I'm starting over. I'm someone different, aren't I? With this realization, I begin to feel a slight rise in my stature. I feel lighter somehow and can feel my spine reaching upward, lengthening like a flower bursting forth from the ground reaching for the sun, anxious to break free from its restraints to unfold freely and show its vibrant colors.

I lift my head and a surge of hope glimmers ever so slightly at the base of my skull, winding its way through the inner darkness. This thin golden thread of light works itself toward my eyes allowing me to see more clearly the path I must take. With renewed strength, a smile begins to form at the corners of my lips that quiver with excitement. My thoughts are interrupted by footfalls on the stairway. It's time. I turn my face away from the window and see my parents coming down the stairs. They walk toward me reaching out to embrace me. Then, pulling back, Mother speaks.

"Madelyn, we need to talk."

"My life is this road

Knowing not where it will take me

But where I could go."

Bryan Farmer

STARTING OVER

Wow! This has certainly been exhausting. Since buying a small pick-up to tote all my belongings, I've been running nonstop. Who knew making a decision to begin again would be the easy part.

The day I left home was difficult for us all. I'll confess I was a bit surprised when my parents approached me with the idea of my leaving. I could feel the imaginary restraints binding me break loose, freeing me to start a new life, seek a fresh environment. I had no idea how in touch they were with my needs. I'm sure it was hard for them, but seeing the relief wash over my face was the confirmation they needed.

I'll always remember them waving anxiously and smiling with encouragement until the very end, until I could no longer see them in my rearview mirror. I'd come to love and respect them for all the sacrifices they'd made for me and I knew their attention was the reason I had faired so well throughout my life. They gave me character and discipline. Without that I could have never survived nor had the courage to move on.

As I traveled further down the road toward my new destination, I felt free and unleashed. I imagined myself emerging from a cocoon, no longer a plain, drab caterpillar but a majestic butterfly with artistically crafted wings transformed with brilliant colors.

A month earlier, I'd been suffocating in my confinement feeling anxious to breathe openly. This imprisonment haunted my dreams causing my lungs to constrict and limiting my flow of oxygen robbing my mind of its freedom to expand in thought.

At last I am exercising my wings, pumping them full of the energy I need, until I can gain the strength to fly unleashed from obligations.

I feel renewed and happy with my surroundings. Landrum, South Carolina is a quaint town, the right kind of place for me. I'm amazed at my good fortune in finding it. Its beautiful scenery and historical buildings are so inspiring. Life has a funny way of pointing you in the right direction, even when you haven't a clue what to do. By opening your mind up to the opportunities around you and letting your inner sense of direction guide you astounding things can happen.

The long drive to get here was fascinating. As far as I knew, I had never traveled anywhere except from the hospital in Maryland to the rehabilitation center nearby and finally to my parent's house in Massachusetts, trips I recall very little of. I was in awe at nearly every turn I took. Driving through the mountainous regions was so breathtaking; the sky a brilliant azure. I was looking forward to the mild winters. I understood that Landrum had only small amounts of snowfall, yet nearby I could journey to the mountains should I feel the need for a New England style snow fix.

It took me two days to get here, stopping overnight at a small inn in Pennsylvania along the way. The next day when I crossed into South Carolina on I-85 south toward Spartanburg, my anxiety level was reaching a peak with roughly thirty more miles to go. When I finally drove into town I could hardly contain myself, for the first building

I noticed to my right was about to become mine — my business and also my home.

I had made the arrangements to lease the building, sight unseen before leaving Massachusetts. Sadly, it was too late in the day to stop by the real estate office, sign the final papers and pick up my keys. I would have to wait until tomorrow to officially become an entrepreneur. I liked the sound of that word. It made me seem important, a real go-getter. I sat in my truck just staring at the building, thinking of all I would do to make it a success. I was also a bit scared, but positive this had been the right step, with any last minute jitters sliding away before taking root. It was perfect!

I drove slowly away and headed up to The Inn, a wonderful little bed and breakfast with a view of Hogback Mountain. Mr. Dobson, the real estate agent I'd been talking with, had recommended it. Upon my arrival, the proprietors, Julie and Hank greeted me with a real southern warmth I'd only read about. They suspected I might be hungry and although it was already past the dinner hour, Julie fixed me a wonderful salad with some homemade biscuits – so good, they melted in your mouth and a small pitcher of peach flavored sweet tea.

The next morning I woke up as the dawn was peaking over the mountains. I sat facing the window imagining what my life would be like here. I had wanted to begin again, start fresh! Well Maddy, I thought to myself you're surely doing that. You don't know a soul here. At that thought, I chuckled to myself. I really don't know a soul anywhere.

I arrived at the Realty Agency the exact moment they were opening to finalize the deal. I was anxious to dig in and get started.

Now my plan is in action and things are coming together nicely. I seem to have melded in thus far. Everyone is curious, but nonetheless the other business owners have welcomed me. They were happy the store was bought instead of sitting vacant detracting from the downtown's appearance. They were also pleased it would remain a bookstore. I had made a decision during the drive in, I would keep my past to myself, sharing only generic glimpses as needed to satisfy folks. Most of those I've met have accepted my reasons for coming to their town without question. I told them I'd been a busy career woman that spent long hours decorating large homes for people with a lot of money, but not a clue about how to furnish them properly. I had tired of the rat race, so when I gently eased into my 50s I decided to escape; leave it all behind to rediscover myself. This wasn't beyond a stretch of the truth since I really didn't know whether I was tired of that life at all; but it made for a plausible story. Most of the people here couldn't imagine living in a big city. Consequently, they readily understood the reasons I gave. Why wouldn't I want to be in this peaceful place? No one prodded or pried further.

I liked that.

NEW SPACES

I moved into the small flat above the bookstore/coffee house I now operate, which will save on costs while allowing me to oversee my business during its first phase. I worried a little about the climb as my back still aches if I overdo it, but then I decided it would give me the exercise I needed daily until the business gets underway and I can take hikes along some of the trails nearby. I purchased some antiques in town and placed a few personal items I'd grown accustomed to from my stay at my parents. Tom sent a picture of me and my parents taken on the day I left the rehab center to head for home and another of him and me from the first Christmas party my parents held that same year. I placed them both in my bedroom as a reminder of how far I've come since then.

I'm sure my parents would be appalled at my moving into something barely bigger than my bedroom at home, but I liked the fact that everything I needed was close by. I suppose this was yet another change from my past since I had grown up accustomed to large spaces and quality furnishings. My Dad was a successful Dentist and my Mother had come from a prestigious family that left her a generous inheritance, which afforded her the opportunity to serve on local theatre and arts committees.

I never thought of myself owning a business, being my own boss – yet I've actually done it. I'm still in the preparation stages, getting ready for my grand opening scheduled to take place in a couple of weeks, plenty of time before the seasonal travelers move on. The store itself is old so it needed a little tender love and care to bring it back to polish. I bought myself a do-it-yourself book and I'm proud to say I've managed to fix some of the floorboards and install a few shelves on my own. I whitewashed the display window to give it a fresh clean look and bought a valance hand crocheted by one of the elderly women in town to hang up above it. I see her walk by from time to time bringing some of her friends to see her handiwork on display, a broad smile beaming across her wrinkled face. It's funny how such a small thing can bring such pleasure to someone. When I saw her come by the first time, I made a silent vow to myself to be aware of other opportunities where simple acts of kindness could lift someone's spirit and to never lose sight of them.

I hear from my parents and Tom, my therapist on occasion. I try to keep them filled in on my activities when possible. I'm not sure I could have done any of this without them. I look forward to their letters of encouragement and support. Their confidence in my abilities sustains me giving me the strength to continue. Especially on days I feel overwhelmed.

I keep forgetting to place an ad in the paper for a part-time assistant. I could definitely use help in getting the stock sorted and set up for display. I've purchased heaps of inventories and I'm anxious to get an opinion from someone else on what I have planned. I make myself a promise to do this tomorrow for sure, no excuses.

Just then, the bell on the back door clangs startling me for a second.

"Hello? Helllloooo, anyone here?" a woman's voice beyond the boxes calls.

I'm sitting on the floor with a pile of books surrounding me. With great effort I stand up to see who it is. Peering over the boxes, I see a very artsy looking woman with a long flowing skirt and oversized shirt, her back facing me. Her hair is long, wildly curly, speckled black and gray. She's attempted to bind it with a leather tie but several strands have managed to escape jutting out at all angles.

"Over here", I holler out, "can I help you?" As she turns toward me I can see she is about my age, perhaps slightly younger with a vibrant smile, her eyes playful.

"Oh! There you are." She turns and confidently walks over to where I am, while reaching her hand out toward me. "I'm Jane," she says.

"Hello, my name's Lyn. I'm afraid the store isn't open yet. As you can see, I'm still trying to organize things. You're welcome to come back in a couple of weeks though. I'm sure you'll find the store in much better shape by then."

"Oh, I'm very excited to see this place open again, but that's not why I'm here. You see, I've been looking for a place to fit in. This store is exactly where I belong. Call it Karma, if you will."

"Forgive me, Jane is it? I'm not sure I understand what you're saying."

"Of course you don't. I always manage to get ahead of myself I'm afraid. You see, I've been looking for work. I live in Tryon, the next town over. Something told me to take a ride to think things through and when I stopped at the light, why your shop was right in front of me. I don't want just any job, but the right job. I think this is it. Oh goodness, I'm stammering again but – I'll just come out with it. Would you happen to need an assistant? I'm very good at organizing things and well, if you don't mind my saying – you look like you could use some help. Am I right?"

Unbelievable, I think to myself, utterly amazing. How could she just drop in my lap like this? Here I've been lax at placing an ad and Bingo – someone shows up – Karma indeed.

Misreading my furrowed brow, she begins again. "Look, that's okay – me and my presumptuous nature barging in again. I'm sorry I disturbed you. I'll let myself out. Please, get on with your work. You must think me an old fool." She turns to go then once more turns back. "Again, please forgive me."

"No-no, please stay. I was puzzled for a moment. You see, I'm always surprised when things work themselves out and the truth of the matter is, I am looking for an assistant. I've been meaning to place an ad, but I'm afraid I have a tendency to put things off. You showing up now – when only a minute ago I was chastising myself for not having followed through is, well – astonishing! I suppose neither one of us should question fate. Let's sit down and talk a while, shall we?"

TEAMWORK

"What do you think about arranging the tables over here, Lyn?" Jane asks the question while she begins moving them to a different spot.

I smile to myself and wonder why she bothers to ask when she'll do it anyway, even without my opinion. I can't complain though, she has a knack for displaying things. I'm not sure how I could have been tops in my field of home design, in my past life. It all seems hard to imagine – too detail oriented for me at this stage. I prefer less stressful activities.

It's been only a week since Jane walked into the store unannounced and already I've realized I could never have gotten this far without her. My eyes nearly popped out of my head though when I watched her leave through the window and saw her walk over to a motor-cycle parked two doors down, hike up her skirt wrapping the sides around each leg, plop a helmet on her head, and roar off. I'd never seen anything quite like it and I wondered what possessed a forty-something woman to select that means of transportation. She was sure to be the talk of the town I'd thought and based on some of the brief whispered conversations I'd overheard in the café down the street since then, my thoughts were accurate.

Later on, while we worked side by side, she told me she had married young and when her husband had unexpectedly died of a heart attack, she decided to do things she'd always wished she'd had time for. Her only daughter was married and living in Chicago at the time so, she decided why not live a little – experiment with life? Although she had been happy being a Mom and wife, she felt she may have missed out on the youthful spontaneous times she could have had. "Now is better than never right? Vvrrroooom!! Vrooom!" she laughed as she turned the gas up on her imaginary handlebars.

She's been a breath of fresh air, even if she does come on a little strong. I kind of like her take over nature, it keeps me on my toes. She's an experimental type too – if she hasn't done it, then she puts it on her list to do. Her list must be quite lengthy by now. Never a dull moment with Jane. She shows me how to have fun, even when we're working.

I'm feeling less anxiety about our Grand Opening next week, thanks to her too. We've been putting in long hours and things are beginning to take shape. I finish placing the last of the coffee cups on the shelf above the counter then turn to see Jane staring at me, hands on her hips, hair wild from the recent flurry of activity with the tables.

"What?" I ask.

"We've done it Lyn. We're just about there. What do you think?"

I still can't believe I'm doing this I think.

"Come On! We need a break", she says and grabs for my hand.

"Where are we going? We can't leave, there's still a lot to do before..." She pulls me along while I stammer excuses.

"We're going on an adventure, Lyn right now. You need it and I need it. We've been working nonstop and I'll bet you haven't been anywhere since you arrived last month, have you?"

"Well…."

"That's just what I thought! Grab a jacket lady, we're going for a ride and put on some sturdy shoes, we may have to climb a bit."

Before we head out, we stop by the café to pick up a couple of deli sandwiches and diet pops, oops I mean sodas. I've already realized a couple of differences from the East coast and the South, one being they don't call soft drinks pop but sodas here in these parts. Jane keeps me aware of my need for nourishment. I have a tendency to forget to eat if I'm busy with other things and since my accident I've been much thinner than I should be.

Next thing I know we're on our way, both of us middle aged ladies busting loose on Jane's Harley headed for the Blue Ridge Mountains just across the state border into North Carolina. We enter a place called Chimney Rock Park and after a short hike along The Outcroppings Trail, we reach a crest referred to as The Chimney with views up to 75 miles – simply breathtaking! We take a seat on one of the benches nearby quietly eating our lunch. As usual, Jane was absolutely right! I have never seen such a glorious sight. The time away from the shop has renewed my energy ten-fold providing the renewed strength of spirit I sorely needed.

My heart is light as we wind our way back down the trail and roar off toward home. I am where I want to be – here in this place – forging my own footpath – leaving my mark.

A HAPPY PLACE TO BE

The business, christened "The Book & Brew" is doing very well, even better than I'd hoped. I attribute much of this to Jane, who is well liked by the customers and full of ideas. She's encouraged me to open up a bit with customers as well, although I still spend a great deal of time observing the people coming here rather than engaging them in conversation. We've been operating for about four months now and already we have our regulars. We try our best to make it comfortable here so people find it easy to sit and relax. The space is fairly small but has a homey feel to it. It's the perfect spot for sipping a great cup of coffee or taking in an herbal tea while reading a book or browsing our bookshelves, perusing the latest novel or magazine. This is what I envisioned it to be – no pressure – no loud noises (unless you count a boisterous laugh or outburst of some sort by Jane) but a happy place to be.

When I'm not making more coffee or ringing up merchandise, I like to walk around and run my hands over the smooth wooden counters remembering how many hours it took to sand away the roughness to get it to this deep beautiful finish. I look at all the shelves filled with so many kinds of books, the types that give you hope, help you cope, let you escape or make you cry. They each breathe a life of their own and I've come to appreciate the pleasure reading has given to me and wonder if the rest of the world views them the same way I do.

Books are what gave me a history again, at least one from a superficial sense. My quest for knowledge kept me focused on living. In the beginning, I learned about others like me, those without memories, but soon ventured into the history of people from all walks of life especially those who had overcome adversity. I was inspired and guided by their voyages, knowing I too was strong enough to find my way again, to make a positive contribution to this life and help others along the way.

I start to ponder the thought of why I had never kept a journal of my life with my family. If I had, perhaps my trek toward remembering or ability to connect would have been a simpler process. There was no point in starting one now though. Who would I leave it to? Who else would care what I think about?

"Lyn, sorry to interrupt, but I could use your help here. The coffee's running pretty low and customers are still arriving. If you could make a fresh pot, I could run out and grab us a couple of sandwiches."

"Sure, Jane" I respond, though my mind is still churning with my latest thoughts. "You know what? I'm thinking of adding a new item. How about we buy some blank journals people could buy, ones to document family trips or hiking adventures, things people do or think about? Do you think they would sell?"

"Definitely, that's a great idea, Lyn. I've always thought about keeping one myself and this location would be a perfect atmosphere to write in. I'm sure travelers passing through would find journaling a great pastime while driving to their next destination also. Here I thought you were daydreaming and instead you're cooking up new ventures. By the way, I have something I need to say", her face now becoming serious. "While it's on my mind…."

I'm not used to seeing her looking quite so sullen and suddenly I'm feeling fearful, so I interrupt her.

"What's this? Don't be getting serious on me; I'm serious enough for the both of us. I need your spunk and energy, Jane."

Seeing the worry on my face, Jane begins to chuckle then reaches out to touch my arm.

"Hold on there, I just need you to know something Lyn, in case you haven't figured it out yet. I'm grateful for you and our friendship. I love this business. I wanted to make sure you knew I'm happy you've let me be a part of it, that's all. Now, that said, I'm off to get lunch!"

Her serious mood changes in a flash. With a bright cheery smile and before I can respond, Jane is out the door in a flurry, making me smile too at my good fortune in knowing her.

COMMUNITY CONNECTIONS

Since the Book and Brew has officially survived, passing the critical one year mark, the town's people are beginning to consider us established. Any caution the shop owners took in getting to know us is now long gone. We've settled into the atmosphere here, keeping true to the small town feel. They've gotten used to Jane's motorcycle roaring into the parking lot in the mornings, falling in love with her good nature and pluck. They've also stopped poking fun at my New England accent.

It helps we've made a practice of giving back to the community as much as we can, if not in dollars, then in our volunteer efforts. We attend monthly community meetings to discuss topics affecting the downtown district, some unusual in nature. Jane's recent favorite was the one about dogs leaving messes in front of businesses and whether or not we needed to provide doggy-do containers alongside the sidewalk, so pet owners can clean up the droppings themselves. It appears Mrs. Greely, owner of the small craft shop in town and one exhibiting a less than friendly attitude toward Jane, had stepped in a smelly pile left near her front door, an event she was none too happy about. Jane had nudged me whispering a sarcastic, *"couldn't have happened to a nicer person"*. We also help pick up trash on clean-up day in the park and donate free coffee to workers at other local events hosted by the Chamber.

The shop is closed on Mondays so Jane and I joined a morning group swim class to boost our aerobic activity without putting stress on our old bones. We didn't realize we would be among the younger to participate. The rest appeared to be seventy or thereabouts, who viewed this class as an opportunity to float idly along while catching up on the latest gossip or ailments of others in the surrounding communities. This is where we met Paige. She started out taking a spot toward the back of the class. We could tell she was struggling to hear the exercises the instructor was suggesting would stimulate the muscles and provide a good workout over the conversations of the older clique. Once, when she asked for a repeat of something she hadn't heard, the other ladies shot her a look indicating her question was disturbing their discussions. Jane and I motioned her to come up near us, but she continued to stay where she was refusing to vacate her position. After a couple of weeks into the class she walked up to us and introduced herself.

"Hello, ladies my name is Paige. How are you enjoying the class?"

"Well, it's interesting", I say.

"If you can hear what's going on and ignore the dirty looks you get when you interrupt the geriatric group's gossip club," blurts Jane.

"Jane, stop it. They just enjoy getting together and talking that's all."

Paige lets go of a small giggle. "I know what you mean. I could see both of you trying to paddle through the Q-tips", she interjects dryly.

I look at her a little puzzled then I hear Jane bust out in laughter.

"Is that what you call them?" She laughs as Paige nods and explains to me by nodding toward them. I turn to look instinctively getting her drift. The group gathered is all quite thin, their white hair poofed out atop their heads. I had to admit they did indeed fit the description.

So this is Paige, very quiet with a wonderfully dry sense of humor. I liked her immediately and so did Jane.

She invited us to her home one day after class, where we shared lunch and talked a lot getting to know one another.

Paige is married though her husband travels with his job and is gone quite a bit. Unable to have children, it has always been just the two of them over the years. She retired recently from a small factory she couldn't wait to get away from. When they offered her a chance at an early retirement, she took it. She's a slightly built woman but packed full of energy for a woman of fifty-two. Jane was surprised to learn Paige lived in Tryon, the same town as she, only Paige lives some distance outside in a wonderful ranch house tucked into the mountains with the most beautiful yard and acreage I'd ever seen. Her flower gardens were full of so many types of plants it would have taken a day to list them all. She also showed us her passion and hobby, which involves creating wonderful arrangements using unusual containers, such as antique coffee pots or glasses. Upon seeing them, Jane and I both had the same thought. Paige would have to join us at the Book and Brew where we could display her creations in our windows and on the tables. To our pleasure, she accepted and we're becoming steadfast friends. That was about two months ago.

Things have been rapidly changing ever since. The customers began commenting right away on the flowers Paige brought in weekly. Some asked if they could purchase them or order arrangements for their own homes. This brought about our most recent enterprise. We set up a display area just outside the entrance. The store sits a few feet below street level with the doorway located along the side of the building by the rear parking lot. There are a few steps you walk down with an alcove approximately three feet by seven feet long. Beyond the door is an area perfect for displaying the flowers and pots. We're adding an open air trestle for hanging baskets also. I suspect this addition will bring about another bit of uniqueness to the shop.

Paige seemed surprised and quite shy about all the attention she's been getting over her pastime, but we see how pleased she is. She never thought her skills would attract such interest, much less be profitable. She had married right out of high school expecting to start a family shortly thereafter, which of course didn't happen. To avoid becoming depressed, she went to work to stay busy. She'd been a laborer packing up widgets blending in with the others she worked alongside. Now she's in high demand with people gushing over her designs.

I close the door locking up for another evening then turn to walk up the back steps to my flat above. I'm enjoying this life of mine. As I begin preparing for bed, I glance over at the mail on my bureau seeing an envelope with a familiar script in the stack. I reach out to pick it up, then place it back down. I'm not anxious to open it feeling guilty for thinking this way but, its mere presence begins drawing me back to a place I no longer want to think about. Here I am, a person suffering from amnesia wishing to forget. How odd is that?

I finish getting ready for bed, lie down and turn out the light. Tomorrow, I'll read it tomorrow.

TOM

I spoke with Maddy the other day about Rose. I wanted to make sure she was handling her Mother's passing all right. She seems hard to reach these days indicating displeasure if I bring up things related to her former life. I suppose she no longer wants reminded now that all her family members are gone.

When I saw her last it was right after Paul, her Dad died. That would have been a couple of years ago, I believe. She had remained vigil in her contact with her parents after her move, though her reactions to them became increasingly distant. She experienced discomfort upon arriving for Paul's funeral. Her distraction was evident with the burden of ghosts unremembered likely weighing heavy in her heart. Maddy was a comfort for Rose that day, arranging to stay at the cemetery with her long after everyone else had departed, while Rose said her final goodbyes to her husband. Her daughter's presence lessened the emptiness Paul's absence created. He had suffered a long time with chronic heart disease but it was the diagnosis of colon cancer a few months earlier that caused his body's rapid deterioration. His illness took its toll on Rose, who insisted on providing much of the care he needed with only a little assistance from visiting nurses. He was 89 then, Rose 85.

I watched over them for Maddy. It wasn't a hindrance to me as I'd grown fond of them during the course of my treatment of her. They were the kind of parents I'd wish I'd had. It also allowed me to remain involved in Maddy's life, filling a small part of it in some way.

When Rose passed away, I'd been out of town and unable to attend her funeral. Since then, I've kept watch over the daughter they so loved. I made sure to stay in touch with her taking over their role, as best I could, her only remaining connection to her past. I didn't want to complicate things any more than they already were for her, thus I've kept my contact minimal. I knew there could come a day when she would remember and she would call on me. She would need her old friend, Tom. I hoped it was soon.

LIVING WELL

Today is June 3, 1991. It's been a decade since the accident that split my life in two. I still cannot recall events from the first part, though pieces hover on the perimeter of my consciousness just beyond reach. I've not permitted this disconnection to stall my progression for the second part of my life. I'm not finished living yet. I don't believe wasting the life one has to be an option even if it would be easier to do so. There are too many pleasures waiting to be discovered so I continue moving toward my future.

The Book and Brew is doing well. I attribute its success, in part, to my good friends & coworkers, Jane and Paige. We work together Tuesday through Thursday from 9:00 a.m. to 7:00 p.m. and on Friday and Saturday from 8:00 a.m. – 8:00 p.m. Sundays and Mondays, the shop is closed allowing us time to explore our other interests and reenergize.

We expanded our coffee bar by adding a light breakfast and lunch menu, keeping it fairly simple. This seemed to encourage our customers to stay in the shop longer to chat with friends or browse the book sections while given the option to enjoy food with their favorite drink. It was a joint effort, each of us contributing our own specialty.

Poor Paige was a reluctant participant in the beginning, I recall. While Jane and I chatted away at the prospects, Paige sat idly by, not joining the conversation.

"What's the matter, Paige" I asked. "Don't you think this will work?"

"Oh, I'm not opposed to the idea at all, but I don't know how I can contribute. I'm not that great of a cook, just average I suppose. The only thing I've been highly complimented on is a little embarrassing to admit."

At this, Jane is all ears prodding Paige to tell us what she means.

"Well, once at a family gathering, everyone began talking about our favorite foods. The conversation led to who made the best casseroles, who made the best cakes, dinners and so on and so on. My husband, overhearing the conversation, pops his head in the room saying – "Paige makes the best toast!" Next thing you know the kids began saying the same thing. "Yeah, Aunt Paige always makes us toast when we stay over and it is the best!"

I'm not sure if it was the forlorn look on Paige's face or the delivery in which she described it, but Jane and I burst into laughter asking her what it was she did so different. She just shrugged her shoulders and said "I don't know but everyone likes it". We assured her toast was indeed a very important and necessary contribution to our menu.

As you may guess, Paige is in charge of making toast and oddly enough, our patrons share the same comment. "You serve the best toast!" Jane and I just smile as Paige shrugs her shoulders with a look of bewilderment on her face.

To compliment our lunch we included a selection of iced coffee and teas with fruit smoothies, popular among younger visitors. All and all it was a good venue to add with the days moving along quickly. This was a blessing to me for reasons not known to most.

Book and Brew

Breakfast Fare
Breakfast Casserole, slice of toast (wheat or sourdough) freshly made each day or fresh fruit

Bowl of fresh fruit

Toast ala carte

Muffins – French breakfast with cinnamon sugar topping; Zucchini Pineapple with walnuts; and, Cranberry Blueberry

Luncheon Fare
Homemade Soups – Creamy Tomato Bisque or Vegetable Lentil

Sandwich Choices – Traditional Egg Salad; Turkey with provolone & cranberry spread; and Chicken Citrus Salad with almonds.

Drinks
Your choice of soda, teas – hot and cold and specialty coffees.

On occasion, Paige and Jane would subtly probe for more historic information of my past, accusing me of being too mysterious. I told them a little of my life growing up based on what I'd been told from my parents. Things like, where I went to school and what I used to do for work. When they asked if I'd ever been in love, I told them I'd been too involved in my career. I did tell them I'd been in an accident since I still had some health issues as a result, but I minimized the extent of my memory loss or any information involving the family I'd lost. I felt a slight twinge of betrayal when I glossed over this aspect of my life, but I didn't want them knowing about this huge gap of blankness. I was fearful the same looks of pity I'd run from before would appear on their faces, and I couldn't take that chance. I told myself it was better this way, things were simpler.

On Mondays, we set aside time to explore together. Occasionally, we went back to the mountains where Jane had taken me on our first lunch so long ago. We often visited the Foothills Equestrian and Nature Center, or hiked along the many trails nearby, like Bradley and Pearson Falls. Landrum itself has continued to keep its traditional small town feel over the years to which I am grateful. Its peacefulness has managed to sustain and lift my spirits daily. I never grow tired of these surroundings I've grown to love so much.

On one particular day, the three of us opted to visit a popular tourist attraction nearby, The Biltmore Estates. The Biltmore was envisioned by George Vanderbilt in 1895, after vacationing in Asheville North Carolina. He was so moved by the beauty of the area, he felt inspired to create an estate in the Blue Ridge Mountains to provide a relaxed and welcoming environment for friends and family. This vision led to a lasting legacy of excellence for Mr. Vanderbilt. The Biltmore, a 250-room family home and country retreat is a top destination for travelers. The on-site Winery produces its own award-winning wines with daily tours an option, culminating in wine tasting at its conclusion. The Winery is the most visited in the United States where approximately 600,000 visitors stop by each year. The Biltmore is also home to acres of formal and informal gardens designed by America's foremost landscape architect, Frederick Law Olmsted. Visitors are encouraged to stroll through the gardens on their own or participate in guided garden walks. In the spring, which is when we visited, the Festival of Flowers is a highlight with a splendid array of color bursting throughout the grounds.

As I'm sure you can guess, Jane's favorite was The Winery. In fact, she had the whole winery laughing by the end of our visit. Each year, the Biltmore creates a special blend that is only available for that particular year and is available for purchase in the estates gift shop. They have a wonderful type of biscuit used to clear the palate between wine samples that was very tasty. We all stood around the tasting area sampling the many flavors and smells of the wines created that season. You can imagine after a few of these samples, heads were spinning slightly, but the mood was light. There happened to be a couple of men, about our age, conducting their own taste-testing at the far end of the bar counter. Glancing their way, Jane asks the bartender if he had any whole limes, and surprisingly he did. Jane asked to borrow one. She picked up her napkin and proceeded to twist the ends tightly while we quizzically watched the process. Plumping up the center, she placed it over top of the lime, concealing it. Next we watched as she rolled it down the counter toward the men. As it passed the other guests they all began to laugh as the "bar crab" sauntered its way down to the men, who when looking up, couldn't help but burst into laughter too. Seeing the three women from whence it had come, they walked over to introduce themselves. One of the men, Ed, took an immediate liking to Jane.

Paige's passion was the Gardens and floral displays at the Biltmore, where classes on container gardening and wreaths are offered. While she was busy learning new techniques to enhance her selections on display at the Book and Brew and while Jane was off getting to know Ed, I found something at the estate that fueled my own desire – history. Storytelling hours took place on the Library Terrace, which is where I was drawn. I was amazed with the tales told by the family as well as friends and acquaintances. It was this contin- ued lasting bond that existed throughout the years by the Vanderbilt family, I admired. The personal grace, strength and determination of Edith Vanderbilt, along with the story of her own upbringing as a child, led to her devotion as a Mother and a wife. It was her steadfast attentiveness to Biltmore and its employees, even after widowed that provided the groundwork of commitment carried out to this day, by her grandson and great-grandchildren.

I couldn't help but wonder if I had been a source of inspiration for my own family in the past, and whether; had they been afforded the chance, would have carried forward any of my strengths or bits of wisdom.

There have been other milestones this past ten years also. I began to volunteer for Homebound Services through the local Library in Landrum. This is a service for people disabled having difficulty leaving their homes. Once a month, I set aside a couple of hours of time to pick up requested items and deliver them to a 90 year old widowed woman on the edge of town. Mrs. Churchill is her name. She is a retired school teacher. She has one son living in Texas with a few grandchildren and great grandchildren living in Charlotte, North Carolina. They try to visit when they can, but everyday life doesn't always provide enough time. She suffered a stroke a few years back and has caregivers come in to assist, but for the most part she functions quite well on her own from a wheelchair.

I end up spending a couple of hours each visit listening to her life stories, always anxious to hear what kind of life others have had and the memories they keep close. One such story centered on her younger years, before she began to teach. She asked me to fetch a metal box on a shelf of her bookcase slightly beyond her seated reach. Handing it to her, she opened it up to show me. It was filled with first place ribbons and other such accolades. She had been a champion horse rider beginning her equestrian career as a child. She suffered a fall in one such event, so severe she lost her courage letting fear of another fall block her ability to continue. She had never competed again distancing herself from the sport and the horses she loved. She had encouraged her students all through her career to never allow fear to get in the way of them succeeding in their lives or stunting their abilities to mature or face those fears head on. Upon her retirement, she decided to practice what she had been preaching and finally face her own fears. She saddled up a horse for the first time in 40 years, at her favorite time of day – as the sun began to crest the hill of the meadow. Feeling the strength of the animal beneath her, talking gently in its ear, she started out slowly, bringing him up to a light cantor, then let him break loose galloping full force, unleashing herself to the passion once again. She rode the fields feeling free for the first time and was returning slowly along a gravel road leading back to the stable when a truck filled with teenagers rounded the bend, its speed far above the limit. The noise and gravel spooked the horse causing it to rear its legs upward and she lost her grip flying into the air, landing on a log at the side of the road which snapped her back in several places. It was this accident that had placed her in her chair forever. I sat stunned. She looked up at me and told me she had no regrets. The decision she'd made had been right and it was the best morning she'd ever had despite its ending. "Some things are worth the risk Lyn", she said. "You remember that."

This story of courage along with other conversations with Mrs. Churchill, led me to another avenue of volunteerism that has brought me a great deal of pleasure.

She told me she'd been watching the children waiting for the bus at a stop across the street from her home in the mornings. She wanted to make sure they safely boarded the bus each day. Her many years as an elementary school teacher gave her insight and the ability to read the faces of the children she nurtured.

"There are many children, Lyn who have a strong desire to learn. You can see it in their eyes, if you really look at them. Many times though, circumstances within their family can hinder their abilities. Sometimes the children become the parent of a younger sibling or often the parent is so lost in their own relationships or lack of nurturing skills the child becomes a crutch they can use toward their own desires. You're a gentle soul Lyn. You could help these children and I believe you might benefit too."

"I don't know, Mrs. Churchill. I'm not sure I could relate to children. I wouldn't know how to approach them."

"Sure you would, just follow your instincts. Give it a try. What do you have to lose?"

She felt sure two of the students she saw waiting at the bus stop would need my help. She even prodded me into arriving early one Monday morning, so she could point them out to me. Of course, I eventually gave in to her wishes not possessing the nerve to disappoint her. I've been enriched beyond belief, as a result.

I will always remember my first little boy, Jay, who was so reserved when we first met. It took several visits before he felt certain I would be there for him, wouldn't desert him. His father had left when he was six years old. At eight, he still felt the pain of abandonment. He had a younger brother, who was five and a little sister only two and a half years old. His mother had given birth to his baby sister only months before his Dad left. His Mom told him it wasn't his fault his father was gone. She tried to explain that his father was overwhelmed with the responsibility of raising a family and frustrated over his lack in keeping a steady job. This information I knew, however, there was something Jay had buried deep inside that still blocked my path, an area I couldn't seem to reach. Shortly before the end of the school year, I gave Jay a small present, a book about a boy and his bike. As I excitedly described the story line, I saw a tear roll down Jay's face causing me to stop abruptly. I placed my hand lightly on his to offer him comfort, not saying a word. I was alarmed at how tense he was, but he didn't pull away so I left it there while he wrestled with an unknown force within. Gradually he began to relax and at last let go of the burden he'd carried since the two years his father had gone.

He told me he had wanted a bike badgering his father for days asking him to please buy him one for his birthday. His Dad hadn't been able to afford one and instead gave Jay a small metal dump truck he'd gotten at a local resale shop. Jay had thrown the toy down running away from his Dad in disappointment. Later on, he apologized to his father telling him he was sorry, and he really did like his gift. A few days later, his Dad left. Jay thought it was his behavior that sent him away. He'd been trying ever since to be a father to his younger siblings, shining shoes and washing cars to earn money, to buy them presents – presents he thought he had denied them from their father. At the end of his story, I gently put my arms around him and held him tight assuring him in a soft voice it wasn't his fault. He was just a little boy. He couldn't be accountable for the action of others. It took a few moments until I felt his small body unwind. He seemed so relieved to finally tell someone.

As the year progressed, he showed a real interest in his assignments. I watched him blossom and by the end of the year his schoolwork had improved greatly. His achievements provided me a satisfaction beyond description and his smile, oh my, what a smile. It is then I knew the rewards Ms. Churchill had spoken of. I only wish I could have told her, but she had passed on a month earlier. I had shared my concerns that I didn't seem to be reaching Jay and perhaps I should let another mentor try. She just kept encouraging me to continue and not give up, for Jay needed me and I must prove my staying power so he could learn to trust me. How right she was, a teacher until the day she died.

I mentored Jay for another two years afterward, until he no longer needed special attention. I would see him in the hallway sometimes when I came to visit other students and he always smiled and waved at me, even when he was with his friends. I would hear them ask him, "Was that your mentor?" and he would answer them saying "Yes, and she's my friend too."

I still have a picture of me and Jay taken on our final session together, given in a Thank You card on Mentor Appreciation Day.

GROWING

"Lands sake, Lyn!"

"What are you talking about now, Jane?"

"I'm talking about this latest creation of yours, that's what! How will I ever regain my girlish figure if you keep putting these temptations in front of me?"

"You may need to be happy with the shape you've got. Sadly, nature has a way of robbing us of our youthful figures, I'm afraid. Your health is a more important factor. Sweets every now and then won't hurt you. Besides, no one's forcing you to eat my cupcakes."

"How can I NOT eat them? People come from miles away to buy these things and you expect me to pass them up when they're right in front of me, within easy reach? What are you calling this one? How about Caramel Fantasy or Tons of Caramel bound to make you weigh a ton?"

"Oh, Jane you're incorrigible", I laugh.

She's right though, even I've picked up a few pounds since I started this new addition to our food line. The tasting, until I got it right, was the biggest factor. Once I finally settled on the recipe's ingredients, with standing ovations from my testers, I hardly ate one for pleasure.

So far, I have twelve perfected recipes concocted little by little over the years. Who would have thought such a simple thing would take off like this?

I remember exactly why I started making them. It began as merely a simple pleasure for my homebound clients, a tidbit to snack on while they read or listened to their books.

My first cupcake wasn't an original. It was similar to one generally found in the supermarket, only homemade, no additives but fresh, moist with the best ingredients. I wasn't concerned about cost as I wanted taste to matter and I wasn't making that many. I made my own version of this popular variety, a delightfully deep, dark, devils food cake with a squirt of butter cream inside, topped with a rich smooth chocolate layer of frosting, plus a few curly cues across the top. I called it *Fudge Surprise*. It was a definite hit and brought back many memories for my clients. I also began bringing cupcakes to the students I mentored each year, as a little treat to celebrate their Birthdays or special holidays. Gradually, I was encouraged to develop others, a variety, which kept them curiously on edge, wondering what kind of cupcake I'd bring next.

I did a twist on the Red Velvet cake, often served in southern communities, by adding a hint of crushed cinnamon candies speckled atop an Italian Butter cream frosting – a Valentine Day delight, the *Red Cinnamon Velvet* cupcake. It was just enough to liven up the original cake recipe a tinge.

Meanwhile, I'd noticed the children at school seemed to enjoy anything gummy these days – Gummy Bears, Gummy Worms, Gummy Fruit. They made quite a game out of the eating process, some sucking on them leisurely one at a time, others chewing them up as fast as they could, their teeth dotted with pieces of color when they smiled. This led to a favorite creation for the youngsters – the

Dirty Worm cupcake. It didn't sound appealing, but it brought smiles to the faces of the kids. Even the adults were sold once they'd had a bite. Eventually, the list grew and grew. The first three became January, February and March followed by:

April	*Nuts to You* – Yellow batter spattered with nutty pieces and a maple & peanut butter chunk frosting
May	*Pink Lady* – Angel food cake with Strawberry Rhubarb frosting
June	*Wedded Bliss* – a champagne cake with vanilla bean frosting.
July	*Lemonicious Raspberry* – white cake with lemon-raspberry glaze
August	*Sassy Root* – scrumptious summertime favorite reminiscent of a root beer float light in taste spouting whipped cream frosting
September	*Cheesy Apple* – spiced apple batter with cream cheese frosting
October	*Jack-o-lantern* – pumpkin cake with orange flavored frosting topped with candy corns
November	*Caramel Delight* – a brown sugar cake batter and Penuche frosting
December	*Cherry Cordial* – a rich milk chocolate cake with maraschino cherry bits topped with a whipped cherry meringue frosting

There you have it, my calendar of cupcakes, a different taste treat to celebrate every month. One might say I've blossomed into a food designer, of sorts.

Because you can't make just one or two cupcakes, I started to sell the extras in the shop. Before I knew it, they were a hit! Customers began buying up all I had. Some wanted them to take as school treats for their kid's classroom; others bought them for work parties. Eventually, I had to increase my baking numbers to accommodate the demand. The fact they were homemade and always fresh, escalated their appeal. Soon the word was out and folks from other towns near and far were traveling in to Landrum to give them a try.

This increased traffic was also good for other businesses in Landrum, as visitors soon discovered the quaint local eateries, antique stores, gift boutiques and even our long-time Betts Hardware store where "you can find anything you need and if you can't, you probably don't need it anyway!", this a direct quote from Mr. Betts the owner.

I marvel to myself as the realization hits me. One small decision, to spread my wings and forge forward so many years ago, has resulted in all this. I wondered less and less of past musings, who I used to be, what I did. My heart feels nearly healed. It's filled with the satisfaction of helping others who struggle with far more obstacles to overcome than I.

RECOGNITION

"Excuse me, can you tell me if Lyn is around?"

"No, I'm sorry. Lyn just left for the store. I'm Paige, is there anything I can help you with?"

"Hello, Paige. My name is Aggie. I work at the Library up the road as the Homebound Coordinator for the program Lyn volunteers with."

"Oh, yes of course. I'm pleased to meet you. Would you like to leave a message for her?"

"Actually, I was hoping I could talk with her, but I suppose you could let her know. Each year our group recognizes an outstanding volunteer and Lyn has been selected as the recipient this year. I wanted to make sure she could attend the awards dinner."

"Wow, that's fantastic. Lyn is one of the most giving persons I know. She's a perfect candidate for your award."

"Yes, that is exactly what the awards committee thought."

"What's going on over here, Paige?"

"Jane, this is Aggie from the Library and she just told me that Lyn is going to get an award."

"Really, how wonderful but you know how Lyn shies away from any compliments. She may be hesitant to attend an event that places her in the limelight."

"You know, you're right, Jane."

"I've got an idea. We won't tell her she's getting the award. We'll surprise her. Is that OK with you, Aggie?"

"Well, I suppose that would be all right. Are you sure you can get her there?"

"You betcha, we can! We'll keep you informed, Aggie. You can count on us."

Jane and I worked out the perfect scheme. We told Lyn we wanted to attend the awards dinner as a ladies night out. She knew of the event, but had never attended as it fell on one of our busiest nights at the bookstore. She gave us some resistance at our suggestion to close early that night, but we convinced her it was a wonderful event, supportive of the local Library, plus we would donate the coffee, tea and some of her famous cupcakes. The townspeople would love the fact we were contributing to a good cause.

We also decided to seek out some of the students she had mentored over the years, as an added surprise. Those we reached were anxious for the opportunity to show their appreciation. The day arrived at last. Trying to go about our regular duties was difficult. I thought sure Jane would spill the beans a couple of times. We both went home a little early so we could spruce up a bit. I hurried back to the shop to make sure Lyn was getting ready. Rushing around the corner, I catch a glimpse of Jane also hustling toward the door.

"What are you doing here, Paige?" she says.

"Oh, you know I couldn't wait any longer. I've been looking forward to this night. I had to make sure Lyn was getting ready so we could be on time."

"What are you two whispering about?"

Lyn is cautiously coming down the stairs. I notice she moves much slower now and I make a mental note to encourage her to move somewhere else, with no steps. The last time I brought it up though she poo pooed the idea saying, "this is my home, and I'm staying until I can't climb at all." I let it go.

"We're not whispering, Paige and I thought it would be nice if we walked over together. Are you ready to go?"

When we enter the hall, we notice practically the whole town has showed up. This is the biggest crowd they've ever had, according to the young girl at the check-in desk.

After enjoying a wonderful dinner, the emcee for the evening introduces the Mayor who will bestow the Volunteer of the Year award.

Jane and I are on the edge of our seat. Tonight, our dear friend will be honored.

He begins by describing the kind of person they look for when searching for this award recipient, the type of qualities they should have and the amount of time they give to others. He then informs the audience that this years presentation is going to stray a bit from its regular format and instead of he presenting the award, there will be a special guest that will do so.

Lyn is listening but not looking directly at the stage. She pours herself a glass of water unaware of the guest walking out on the stage. As she places the pitcher down on the table, she hears the Mayor's announcement.

"Please join me in welcoming, Jay Prescott."

Lyn looks up to the stage amazed. "Jay", she whispers.

From the side of the stage, a handsome young man, makes his way to the podium. Extending his hand to the Mayor, he utters a Thank You, and then quickly turns his mouth toward the microphone.

Without hesitation, he speaks in a clear voice – "Good evening. It is my utmost pleasure to present this award for Volunteer of the Year, to the person who has had the greatest impact on my life, a person who gave me courage to face my fears and move forward in a positive direction, my mentor and my friend, Lyn Grayson. Before, I go on I'd like to ask her to come join me."

A shocked Lyn rises never once turning her gaze from Jay. She makes her way up to the stage, while the audience stands applauding, some touching her arm in congratulatory gestures. When she reaches the podium, Jay bends down to hug her holding her tightly for a few moments, affording her the chance to regain control of her emotions before she must speak. He then turns to the audience, his arm still encircling her shoulders.

"Ladies and gentlemen, if you know Lyn, you need no explanation from me on why she's been chosen for this award. It was with her encouragement through the "Let's Learn Together" mentoring program at my elementary school that made me what I am today. I graduated from college, the first ever in my family to do so, and an accomplishment I would have not thought possible years earlier. I became an elementary school teacher. Lyn not only emitted patience when helping me with my schoolwork, she gave me a piece of herself each and every time she sat coaxing me along. She wasn't the kind of person that volunteered to make her self feel good. She volunteered because she wanted to give us something we could use in our lives, instill a spirit of pride when we had so little esteem. She taught us respect for ourselves and others. She taught us to face our challenges and be strong. She also helped me understand what compassion is and how our mistakes can be used to help us learn and grow. She was always there, never missing a session, brightening our lives on special days not only with her smile, but with a small cupcake seasoned with love."

As Jay spoke changing his inflections from himself to us, the stage began to slowly fill with other students whose lives Lyn had touched over the years until they stood alongside and behind her, ten in all. As Lyn noticed them gathering, she walked over to hug each one of them. When she had acknowledged them all, Jay stepped away from the podium allowing Lyn to move forward. She glanced over, as the students joined together at the side of the stage and before she could speak, they honored her one more time with their own personal applause.

I watched her breathe in deeply, taking a moment I suppose, to gather her thoughts, regain her composure. Then with a flair only Lyn possesses, she blew us all away when she spoke.

"First off, I want you all to know how grateful I am to be honored in such a way. However, I also feel the need to put such things in perspective and address this question. What is the importance of being significant? I'd like to quote parts of a message, I heard on the radio one day, by Dr. Rex M. Rogers entitled – Making a Difference. It goes something like this:

"Many of us have pored over the obituaries and read of individuals whose accomplishments are so impressive, many of us feel lacking – the World's Richest Man, the WWII Medalist, Inventor or Former Vice President Laid to Rest. Although this list of Who's Who may be remarkable, the world marches on and their time in the sun is quickly forgotten. What chance than do the rest of us have for lasting significance? What adds significance to our lives? Does it come from within us? If so, we're still in trouble, because people with exemplary spirits are also soon forgotten."

"Significance then must come from something outside of us, something that provides a point of unchanging reference. The Bible teaches us that our significance generates in our source as created beings made in the image of an eternal, Sovereign God. Because God is, and because He loves us, all human beings possess dignity and everlasting significance. Thusly, we may never be a "Who's Who," but more importantly, in God's eyes, we will never be a "Who is he or she?"

Having said this, Lyn thanked everyone once again and walked off the stage, leaving us all feeling honored in ourselves and in knowing her, as only she could do. It took a full five minutes for the clapping to subside.

ENLIGHTENMENT

I opened the shop today, the same as all the other thousands of days, only this one wouldn't end the same at all.

"Jane, could you hand me that spoon over there?"

"Sure, hon. Here you go. What kind are you making today Lyn? Please say it's nonfattening – puhleeeeeeeese (stretching out the word for emphasis)?"

As I take the spoon from her and smile, I hesitate a bit before I tell her they're her favorite (she loved the name) – *Nuts to You*. I make sure to add that nuts are fiber and fiber is good for you, trying to soften the impact of what I know will cause her to go off her diet once again. I'm making the maple peanut butter frosting for the last cupcake batch I left cooling last night, too tired to finish until this morning. I need to be quick, as our doors will open soon, bringing in the first customers of the day.

We came out with a 2005 calendar for the Book n Brew, shortly before the Christmas holidays highlighting pictures of the twelve cupcakes – one for each month. This seems to have heightened the number of sales, as a result. Although I make several kinds each month, *Nuts to You* happens to be the April cupcake. There-fore, I'm preparing for an onslaught of requests for this particular one. Everyone loves Peanut Butter. It seems the locals rely on the monthly rotation. It makes me wonder if they place reminders on their refrigerators, in office calendars or other electrical devices to alert them to the kind of cupcake under production. Those that don't remember, call the shop merely for that reason. "What's Lyn making this month?" they ask. I do love pleasing them all and nowadays I only make what I can without over taxing myself. When they're gone, they're gone, I tell them. We've learned to prepare ourselves for Tuesday mornings by splitting the baking into Sunday evenings and a little more on Monday mornings when we're closed.

I'm aging so I'm slowing down some. I try to keep things light not too demanding. Work is becoming more difficult these days. Even Paige, a few years younger than I, stopped taking flower orders for weddings and other big events. She only creates a few arrangements to sell outside the shops entrance and fills the vases on the tables inside each week. Her husband retired last month so she'd like to take advantage of his being home now – to settle in and grow old together.

Jane and Ed ended up getting married about five years back and they moved into a small condominium just outside of Asheville near The Biltmore where they met. Ed is talking of retiring soon and I know Jane wants them to spend time traveling, while they still can. She's hesitant to tell me she wants to retire, too. I think she's afraid of leaving me alone with everything. She's been a part of this from the beginning. We've journeyed a long way together, we're family. I've thought over my next steps and I have a plan underway.

The bell on the door rings, interrupting my thoughts. I hear Jane and Paige talking, then another voice I don't recognize. I place the last of the cupcakes on the tray and head out front to place them in the case.

"Lyn, there's someone here to see you, says she is an old friend of your family. I told her you would be right out. She's standing over there, with her boys." Jane gestures toward the children's section.

As I begin walking toward her I am wondering who this could be and would I even have a clue as to whom it is, that was friends of my family and which family she means. I feel my heart quicken. I slow my steps down and as I do, I can't help but overhear their conversation.

"Oh come on you two, stop teasing one another. Eli, quit!"

My attention focuses on the boys – one blond the other dark and for a split second, there is a flash of recognition in my mind. Images of two other boys come into view. I can see them sitting on the floor pushing each other playfully, grabbing for a small toy of some kind and suddenly I am seated in an overstuffed chair. I feel the softness of the cushions enveloping my body, my legs tucked up next to me. I have a book in my hands and I glance to make sure the boys are just playing, not serious in their arguing. I can smell a clean saltiness in the air, perhaps the ocean? I can't put my finger on it then I am back in the bookstore. I feel as though the blood has drained totally out of me, causing me to sway ever so slightly. It is at this instance the woman turns and sees me.

"Oh my goodness, are you OK?" she says reaching to steady me.

Jane and Paige too are quickly at my side. Evidently, they were watching me approach the woman their curiosity involving someone from my past peaked.

I allow them to lead me to a table nearby. I sit down trying to collect myself and shake off this feeling. I see the boys looking at me, quieted by this episode of mine and wondering if this old person is going to die in front of them. I already imagine them telling their friends all about it as young children will when they see something unusual occur, stretching the truth as far as they can to make it sensational and emit jealous envy from their friends.

"Settle down, settle down. I'm fine. I just blanked out for a minute. Don't worry yourselves. I'm not checking out just yet." I flash the boys a quick smile and I'm not sure if I see relief or disappointment, as I'm robbing them of their tall tale.

"Please, have a seat with me and tell me what brings you here", I say to the woman.

Jane and Paige now assured I'm truly OK, hurry back to the counter to get ready for the breakfast crowd.

"Let me explain, the woman says. You're Maddy, right?"

"Well, yes" I say. "People here know me as Lyn though. I was starting out fresh and well, the name change just seemed the right thing to do."

"All right, Lyn it is. My Mother was a friend of yours when you were growing up in Massachusetts. She said you used to be very good friends all the way through high school and even after until…"

She stops then seeing me glance toward the counter to make sure no one was listening.

"Well, you know what I mean. The thing is – I only wanted to say Hello. I'm Alexa Martin. My mother's name was Sara Royce. These two ruffians are my twin troublemakers, Eli & Sam." She ruffles their heads playfully. "When I was little, my mother used to tell me about some of the things you and she did growing up. I loved hearing her stories. It was a special time of sharing "just between us girls" she would say and I liked that I knew something about my Mother my brothers weren't part of."

"One day, I happened to read an article about your famous cupcakes, not realizing the connection. I showed her the article thinking it a novel idea. A picture of you holding a tray of your cupcakes happened to be next to the article and my mother recognized you instantly. She said she had wondered where you had gone and even then, she still missed your friendship. I told her maybe someday we could travel this way and perhaps you could reconnect. Unfortunately, she passed away a few months later, a sudden heart attack."

"I'm so sorry, dear, only it may have actually been more upsetting if we had talked again. You see, I still don't remember a thing about that time in my life."

"I see" she said. "I hope my visit isn't causing anguish for you, only I felt compelled to come here. You know to say Hi, for my Mom. She really valued the part you played in her life and I thought meeting you might – "

I watch her brush away a small tear trickling ever so slightly from the corner of her eye. I pat her hand gently.

"No of course not, I've come to terms with my memory loss. I'm no longer frightened of my past dear. I wish I could share in her memory with you, but it isn't anywhere I can reach yet."

We sit silent for a few minutes gazing at the boys who have quietly begun entertaining themselves with one of the game boards I keep handy for guests to use. Watching them, I am again taken over by a strange feeling of familiarity and I struggle to find more in the hiding places of my mind, to see if I can understand why.

"Well, Alexa, I finally say. I'm glad you came by just so I could meet you and your boys. I don't often run into folks from the East coast anymore and it's wonderful you took the time to come here. I'm certain your mother would be pleased. Now! I'm sure you'd love to try one of my cupcakes, right? Come on boys, I'll let you try the Dirty Worms I sell here."

"Ewwwuu! You sell dirty worms to eat?" they say in unison, faces distorted in disgust.

Alexa and I both chuckle.

"You just wait boys, you're gonna love them, you'll see."

MADELEINE MOMENTS

Time Lost, Time Regained
An excerpt from a Marcel Proust novel, In Search of Lost Time
(*Adapted from Swann's Way, Remembrance of Things Past*)

"And suddenly the memory returns. The taste was that of the little crumb of Madeleine which on Sunday mornings, when I went to say good day to her in her bedroom, my aunt Leonie used to give me, dipping it first in her own cup of real or of lime-flower tea….. And as soon as I had recognized the taste of the piece of Madeleine soaked in the decoction of lime-blossom which my aunt used to give me, immediately the old grey house upon the street, where her room was, rose up like a stage set … and with the house the town…the streets along which I used to run errands, the country roads we took when it was fine … the whole of Combray and its surroundings, taking shape and solidity, sprang into being, town and gardens alike, from my cup of tea."

DISCOVERY

The memory light has come on and I wish it hadn't. It would be easier if I could simply flick a switch. Click, I forget again or maybe click, that makes me feel good so let's remember that day. I hadn't realized how comfortable the darkness had become or how far I had lapsed into complacency. After twenty-five years I begin the grief process for a life long lost, forgotten. I feel as if I've reached a milestone, one I'd rather not have conquered. Unlike the satisfaction experienced when celebrating a silver Wedding Anniversary, which in this day of quick escape and self adulation is quite an accomplishment. I wonder whether it's a blessing to finally know or if I'm being punished for something I've done wrong.

These tiny glimpses into my past began while I slept. There were no faces I recognized, only feelings that crept over me. Short snippets of a faceless man, of small silhouetted children playing on a beach, an old house in the distance, cookie smells fresh from the oven – all left me curious to know more. The memories came like short jolts of electricity coursing through my body, awakening neurons in my brain from somewhere deep within. I imagined them casting light in areas where earlier only darkness prevailed. With each corridor they entered, the webs and shadows began to fall away until my head was so full, I thought sure it would burst. A sense of calm prevailed upon my awakening. I was never unsettled or distraught, but satisfied and happy – somewhat comforted by an unknown presence. It had all begun the evening following Alexa Martin and her twins' visit.

My mother had kept boxes of my past keeping them stored safely until the time I would want to look inside. She never gave up hope I would regain my memory and the items she'd packed would help bring pleasure along with closure. She spoke to me of their importance, making me promise to keep them because someday I would be glad I had. Out of respect, I honored her request in the event she was right. The pictures I'd seen years ago had certainly signified a happy existence. There was no escaping the broad smiles on all our faces. Who was I to destroy such a history? I may have moved on and started another life, but I wasn't so self assured I could deny I'd been another person. Albeit, a person who had suffered a great loss, even though unaware how severe or tortured that loss had been. I wished she was here now, so I could let her know I remembered her. My heart aches with the knowledge I can never give her that simple joy she so craved.

I reach for one of the boxes. I stare for a long time at the yellowed tape attempting to secure it. Its stickiness is no longer apparent, now brittle with age. My hand begins to move forward on its own seemingly independent of my mind and body. I'm afraid of what I will view inside, yet I know it's time. As the pieces of tape easily break away, I lift the flaps then remove the newspaper covering its contents. When I look downward a small gasp escapes me. It is a picture of two boys, one blond the other dark. Instantaneously, I know they are my sons – Ian and Jon.

I begin to softly weep.

FLOODED THOUGHTS

On the evening I began delving through my past, I was awake most of the night. Once the memory doors opened, they began unraveling aimlessly at a rate too fast to grasp. There were scenes I was unable to decipher, blurred like a poorly focused photograph. I've heard people say, when a person is dying, their life flashes before them in an instant. I began to wonder if I had actually died and didn't know it. I was afraid to sleep fearful I would lose everything regained, yet fearful I would not. Eventually, I collapsed from exhaustion, memories scattered around me like confetti.

When I awoke, my head was aching from the conflicting emotions coursing through me. My eyes were red, swollen from tears of both happiness and sadness. I felt I was spinning futilely, no longer able to concentrate on even simple things. I struggled to recall what day it was. When it came to me, I breathed a sigh of relief. Thank goodness, it was early Sunday morning and the shop is closed. I look at the objects strewn around me, my eyes falling again across a letter from my Mother and the news article lying nearby.

I reach for the phone. There's only one person I can rely on to help me handle this. He's the only one who knows. I dial the familiar number and while the phone rings, I look around at the life surrounding me. The answering machine picks up. At the sound of his voice, I begin to sob leaving a garbled message. "Please call Tom, please." I place the receiver back on its cradle than slowly begin to crumble.

Lying there, I am transported backward to a winter scene. I see myself standing alongside my father, who is seated at a small bench. We are inside an enclosure of some kind, a tent I believe. I'm staring down into a small hole filled with a dark liquid. I can feel the coldness, numbness on the tips of my fingers. As the image clears, I remember the day. My father had taken me ice fishing at a lake close to our home. It was the first and last time, I went. I was around six years old. As I continue to watch the scene unfold, I see a fish coming to the surface. My father lifts it up proudly for me to see. I stare at its bulging eyes, its gaping mouth, its gills opening and closing, searching for the water it needs to sustain it. My father grasps its body and begins to remove the hook from its mouth, tearing a bit of its flesh as he does. There is red fluid dripping from the rip. He places the fish on the ice and turns to reach for the bucket he brought, to carry it home in. I stand still watching as it flops on the ice, desperately looking for a solution, a way out to avoid its fate. I am enthralled by its beauty, even as it lies dying. The colors of its skin are vibrant against the stark whiteness of the ice. My thoughts are interrupted as a loud ringing pierces the air. I hesitate – not wanting it to be Jane or Paige right now. I try blocking out the sound looking for an escape, much like the fish on the frozen pond. Finally, I take the plunge, picking up the receiver.

"Hello?"

"Maddy, it's me, Tom! What's happened? Are you OK?"

All I can say is – "It was me, Tom. I killed them."

I lapse again into a distant fog. In the background, I hear him saying to hold on. He is coming.

TOM

It's not uncommon for a therapist to arrive home from a trip to find their message light blinking. It's also not uncommon to push the button while continuing to sort through a stack of mail, start unpacking, fix a drink or perform any other typical household task, as you listen to them run through. When the voice came on the machine, I stopped midtask. I quickly went to the phone to dial the number, my heart beating rapidly. It's time. I knew instantaneously, the missing pieces of her life had returned. The message confirms something else. She was aware of a fact she'd never been told – one sure to shake her up a bit.

When she answers, I know what must be done. I am explicit in my instructions saying exactly what needs to be heard.

"I'm coming. I'll be there before the day ends. Focus on the good times, accentuate the positives. Remember the beach house."

I hang up the phone praying she understands, repack my bag and rush out the door.

MADELYN

OK, I tell myself. Focus. Tom mentioned the beach. I should remember the beach. I rifle through the snapshots finding one of Neil and me on our wedding day, taken on a beach. I close my eyes and try to conjure the day in my mind. I breathe slowly, in and out – in and out – following the methods of Memory recall I was instructed on, many years ago. Depend upon your feelings, smell the sight, hear the wind, don't focus on language only the image and the place – draw yourself backward, open your mind and collect the pieces. Once again, I am caught up in the scene, as though I've hit rewind on the video recorder allowing me to relive the moment a second time.

I remember driving along the coastline, my car top down, the music of an Eddie Heywood tune, Soft Summer Breeze is playing on the radio.

I felt great, young and ready to face the world. I was working at Tackett Creations, a design firm in Connecticut, starting shortly after graduating college, three years earlier. It was the first time I'd been given sole discretion in deciding how a house would be decorated. I felt especially honored with the assignment as the house was the product of a well known architect, Neil Grayson.

I'd been told he was particular about how the houses he designs are transformed with décor, so I'm a little nervous. He takes care in positioning the houses at a proper angle in relation to the surrounding landscape and view, which is why many wealthy persons pursue his talents. He even follows the process through, by meeting with the interior design firm on its plans for furnishings, assuring the customer an inclusive formation. His rooms are laid out with a particular feel for the items placed inside. He only works with clients who understand and can appreciate his methods. His level of success commands respect, another reason his designs are sought after. It's rumored he leaves a signature mark somewhere inside the house, challenging the owners to locate it. As far as I know, no one has.

I also decorate a room by feel first, which is why I don't bring sketches beforehand. I walk into a room and close my eyes, opening up to the sounds it makes, the senses it generates from within. I focus on lighting, outside views and the personalities of the people who will live there.

Pulling my car into the driveway I see him standing on the porch. He's looking toward the ocean. The house itself is no less than spectacular and I feel paled by its beauty. Its contours gently follow along the setting in which it's been placed, not drawing attention to the house alone but the entire scene that contains it. I'd seen pictures earlier, yet none captured the image that lays before me now.

"Well, don't just stand there," he says reaching out his hand. There's more you will want to see. I'm Neil Grayson. You must be the decorator the Wynnes have hired, yes?"

"Yes, I'm Madelyn Weber. It's a pleasure to meet you, Mr. Grayson. I'm very pleased to be working with you. I mean it's an honor to…"

He interrupts my stammering with a lighthearted laugh. "Please, don't shower me with your praise or it may go right to my head. Call me Neil and relax, Maddy. Is it all right, if I call you Maddy? It seems to suit you, don't you think?"

"Now you're stammering," I say, smiling broadly.

"Yes, I suppose I am."

As my memory fades away, I mentally return to my room, a smile still lingering across my face.

So this is love. This was our beginning. How could something so special hide within me for so long? Love truly lifts the spirit, changing a person in seconds. I hadn't realized how large the void in my heart was.

How wonderful it feels to set that missing piece of the puzzle securely into its rightful place – a perfect fit.

With the warmth still permeating my body, I stand up to stretch. I feel different somehow – loved I guess. Its early afternoon and I haven't veered from this spot. I decide to make a cup of tea hanging on to loves comfort. I step gingerly around the pictures without seeking more of their history. I need time to gather my thoughts, regain control. I draw upon the strength that has carried me this far. Setting aside the invading images as best I can, I proceed to the kitchen, placing the kettle on the stove. I busy myself with selecting a brand of tea, chamomile perhaps. Knowing I should eat something, I grab a banana. I peel away the skin slowly, concentrating on the task with every movement of my hand. Taking a bite, I focus on the chewing with the same absorption. Any break in my attentiveness could send me backward once again. As I walk to the bathroom, I take small sips of my tea. I turn on the shower, remove my clothes then enter the steamy enclosure. As the water cascades along my body, I strive to keep the memory of Neil and me together, alive within me. If I hang on tightly, I can make it through the next couple of hours until Tom arrives.

Stepping out of the shower, I feel renewed. Water always affects me this way, whether I'm showering, soaking in a tub, drinking it or merely looking at it. It has the power to alter my mood, in a positive way. I look at my reflection in the mirror. I am seventy-three. The lines on my face seem to have deepened overnight and I find myself following along its creases with curiosity. It's been some time since I looked at myself so intently. I've never concerned myself with the years passing, choosing instead to wrap my thoughts on days, individually rather than looking back on them collectively and wondering where they'd gone. Perhaps losing my past caused this fore thinking. After all, what's done is done.

Now with a return of memory, I feel I've been granted an opportunity to experience my youth once again, like reading through a journal, I never thought to keep. I let my mind begin to drift toward the beach once more.

Neil and I are sitting on the sand watching our children play along the edge of the water. They are still small, Lucy around eight and the twins – Ian and Jon a few years younger. They are running forward chasing the water as it recedes, then scurrying backward quickly to escape its wetness as it now chases them.

We laugh at their playfulness marveling at our good fortune in being blessed with such beautiful children – so full of life.

Except now they aren't, I think and the sadness begins to creep in, pools of water forming in my eyes.

My feelings fluctuate up and down like a seesaw. How do I grieve 25 years late? How do I muster up a loss long gone, into one evicting sadness fresh and new – especially when memories recalled are so sweet? Can I cloud up my existing life with the past when this life anew has fostered me such comfort? How do I accept responsibility for past wrongs when I've accomplished so many rights?

Although these two periods are vast in difference, they will soon complete me in a way I never knew was missing.

I take a deep breathe wondering if I have time to take a walk, when I hear the bell ring at the door below.

TRUTHS CAN SET YOU FREE

Tom is standing by the door, pacing back and forth. His hands are in his pockets, head tilted downward. He's aged considerably since last I saw him, I think. Same as I, I suppose. As I open the door, he looks up – his familiar smile spreads across his face.

"Maddy, how are you doing?" he says reaching his hand out to greet me.

"Oh Tom, I'm so glad you're here." I bypass his hand and give him a hug. We are friends, not only patient and therapist, so I feel comfortable extending this personal greeting.

"Come in, please. I know you've had a long drive. Would you like something to eat or drink?"

"Not necessary, Maddy. I picked something up along the way. I'm more concerned about you right now. Let's have us a talk, Okay?"

I show him upstairs to my apartment and begin filling him in on everything I've remembered thus far – sticking closely to the good memories, avoiding the one that prompted me to call him here.

A couple of hours later, he begins to lay out his plan for our weekend. We talk about some of the conflicts I've had over the years such as; the guilt I've experienced in leaving my parents behind to start again, when they probably needed me near them; along with my periods of self deprecation at my failure in remembering my husband and children. He assures me that when the truth is finally recognized, I can begin my final recovery. He goes on to say the recovery process must be approached systematically involving three specific steps, which he intends to follow. Because of our past sessions and friendship over the years, our first step together is much easier than it would be under a new therapist to patient relationship. I know Tom and trust him therefore he's already established a comfort zone with me, an aura of safety. The fact we are proceeding with this treatment, inside my own apartment is also safe for me. At this point, he asks me one final question before he continues.

"Maddy, you need to tell me how much you remember about the day of the accident."

"I only know what was written in the letter my Mother left for me. She said I had been driving when the accident occurred. Realizing I was responsible for everything caught me off guard and the impact sent me in a tailspin. I robbed them of life, Tom – Me! I didn't want to know anymore so I tried to block it out again, but this time I couldn't. Then, I called you." My hands begin to shake and the tears stream freely. He places his arm around my shoulder letting me cry away my sorrow.

"Ok, Maddy. I know this is difficult, but it's important to move forward. What I need to know now is – Are you ready to face this? You're the one in charge. It's you, who has to get through it. I can only help you along the path. I believe this is what you want or you wouldn't have called me. Am I right?"

"Yes – yes, it's time but I can't do it alone."

"Then let's begin. I need to fill you in on what I was told, by your parents and the police.

Tom proceeds to tell me why the details of the accident were kept quiet. Since my absence of memory failed to supply an emotional connection to my family, I never really pursued the specifics surrounding the accident. There could be no comprehension or acceptance for my role in this tragedy, without these feelings. I had to know them in order to mourn them, he said.

"Now, for the hard part", says Tom. "You must be ready to confront the accident head on, Maddy. Everything you can remember – in depth – in detail. You can't hold anything back no matter how painful it becomes. Make yourself comfortable close your eyes if you like. Focus fully on the moment. Maybe you could start, by trying to remember the circumstances leading up to the events, placing you at that exact spot. What you were doing earlier, before you got in the car. I'll be right beside you. You can rely on me, Maddy. I'll help in any way I can."

I'm afraid, yet I know what I must do. Despite my hesitancy in burrowing deeply within my mind, I feel the necessity to open up my wounds. Who am I to avoid suffering, when my family paid the ultimate price for my error?

I close my eyes cognizant of the monster I will face. I'm a strong woman, I tell myself – older, more fragile than before, but still strong, a trait I now know was passed along from my Mother. I reach my hand out and as I know he will, he takes it between his own. I can draw from his strength too. I am aware of what I mean to him. I've always known, but we both have understood, friendship alone was our limit. As I start to unwind, my memory begins to recall images. Slowly, the picture within gains clarity, though I struggle to recall, where I am. I finally realize I am seated at my work desk, papers strewn across it. They appear to be sketches of rooms in a house, with splashes of color added here and there. I begin to talk aloud, describing to Tom what I'm seeing.

"I think I must be in my office, at work. I'm going over some papers, most likely design concepts for one of the houses I'm decorating. There is a day planner sitting in front of me. I was always making notes, writing things down to make sure I didn't forget the things I needed to do. The date is June 3, 1981. That's the day of the accident, isn't it?"

"Yes, Maddy. Keep going, what else do you remember about that day?"

"I was supposed to pick up Neil from a house he was working on, in Worcester I think. He must have been on a job, which explains why I was driving. Next, we're supposed to pick up Lucy, Ian and Jon from school. We were going on vacation, to the beach. I remember this was likely to be the last time we'd have a chance to vacation together. Lucy had just completed her degree and would be focused on her career – begin her own life. She had recently accepted a job in advertising with a company in Boston and was hunting for an apartment there – leaving home completely. She was so excited to be spreading her wings, looking forward to her future and being on her own.

Children are always looking to be further along in life, wanting to be older than they are, until suddenly they find themselves no longer young. I suppose we all have a tendency to do this, when growing up though. It's hard to live in the moment.

We are in the car now. Ian and Jon are teasing Lucy about something. They're all laughing, including Neil. I remember thinking how lucky we are to actually enjoy each others company – not every family can boast of such an accomplishment.

As we travel down the highway, the clouds begin to roll in and the sky darkens. The rain begins sporadically, but as we continue the darkness deepens and the rain's intensity grows. I have the wipers on the fastest speed, the sound deafening as they bang back and forth and still they barely clear the glass for me to see — a windshield waterfall. The cars are moving slower up ahead, but faster than I like. I maneuver to the right lane. I'm nervous, concerned with the number of cars on the road, my knuckles tense turning white as I grip the wheel. I tell Neil I'm going to pull off at the next exit, until the weather improves. He agrees it's a good idea, saying he will drive, when we begin again. There are flashing lights on the shoulder ahead to the right of me, a truck appears to have pulled off the road. I slowly guide our car to the left to allow us to drive by, with some distance between us and the stopped vehicle. The truck starts to reenter the highway just in front of me, at the same time I continue moving over. As I approach, I'm cognizant of the back wheels of the truck, when without warning the car floats across a film of water, careening sideways. I'm powerless to stop its momentum, as the back of the car clips the wheel of the truck. Like an old black & white film, I see each click of the slide, the quality poor with scratchy white lines cutting through them. The top of the car folds in on itself, soft as a piece of plastic wrap – my son, Ian's voice saying – Mom, only I can't determine if he's trying to alert me to the danger or merely uttering it one last time. I'm sure it's a matter of only a few seconds, and then I'm out while the car parks its self – backed into a cave underneath the bed of the truck. I recall waking up briefly, while I am still trapped in the vehicle, my eyes resting on Neil's legs – puzzled by their positioning. At the same instance, I am alerted to an intense pain, permeating my body. When it escalates higher and higher, until I can no longer hear myself scream, I dive off into a darkened pool of oblivion.

Above the perimeter of my head, I hear voices and a disturbing grinding sound, which annoys me. I try to shut it out, but it keeps repeating itself with sudden ear piercing pops. I feel a release of pressure against me, then tugging. It brings to mind the time I was at the dentist having my tooth extracted — the push and pull of the forceps, gripping the tooth then the release of the roots, snapping one at a time in my gums – no feeling of pain, only an invasion taking place in my mouth.

I vaguely remember the sensation of wheels rolling underneath me, lights flashing back and forth across my eyes, my arms and legs moving beyond my control — strung up like one of the marionettes in the library the children loved to watch on Saturday afternoons. Nothing more, until later when I hear you, Tom and my parents talking in my room." I open my eyes while exhaustion consumes me.

"Describe what you're feeling right now, Maddy."

"I'm not certain I can, but — I guess besides being tired, the closest way to describe it is; empty, like I've pulled a plug and everything inside me has drained out on the floor around me. I believe I understand what they mean, when people describe someone whose lost everything as a 'shell of themselves', it's difficult to define. I'm devoid of emotion, which is odd. I should feel remorse, sadness or anger at the least. Shouldn't I feel something?"

"I believe what you're feeling is quite normal. You've opened up many closed doors, Maddy. The fact you're detached means you can separate yourself, look squarely at what happened. Although a tragic incident, it's only a part of a whole. Our lives are made up of pieces, events that occur over time. You will think of this one every day, for as long as you live and you'll grieve every day as well, but over time this grief will lose its vividness, falling into place alongside all the happy times you've recaptured, to relive over and over. You may have been behind the wheel Maddy, but it wasn't your fault. There was nothing anyone could have done. You had planned to exit the safest way possible and Neil had agreed to that plan – circumstances didn't allow it to happen. None of us can explain why bad things occur to good people – they just do. Let yourself embrace your family again – know who they were – take pleasure in what you had together. All the memories are there now or soon will be – look at your life and see what a wonderful life it's been, before and now."

"Tom, do you think I could be alone for a little while? I'd like to look through more pictures, by myself."

"Of course, Madelyn I need to check into a room in town for the night, then I'll stop back by for a bit to make sure you're all right. There's one more thing I've brought, I think you may like to see now."

He reaches for an odd shaped box and hands it to me. Inside I see a small projector along with reels of tape. I look up at him quizzically.

"Your parents asked me to keep these until the right time came. You know, they never gave up hope that one day you would remember. For more than 20 years you and your family vacationed at the same spot, renting the same beach house on Nags Head Island. It became a tradition, brimming of special memories. These tapes are a history of those years, your chance to see them in life – watch them grow again."

I cannot speak. My hands clasp his, while I lift my reddened eyes toward him, filled with gratitude. The thought of seeing them in life, gives me hope in erasing my last and final view. I reach inside, barely conscious of the click of the door, as it closes behind him.

SECRETS REVEALED

It was a bittersweet goodbye this afternoon when Tom left for home. His friendship has given me the sustenance I needed to complete my recovery, of which I am forever grateful. I care deeply for Tom but his role in my life has served its purpose and now my family had come back. I could tell he was happy for me but saddened for himself, as his patient has made the final journey toward closure. The thread that connects us has grown thin and although we will stay in touch, I doubt we will ever see each other again. The battles we've fought have produced wounds too tender – too prone to opening, inflicting new pain. Tom has finished his job, yet in doing so he knows he must move on. He is foremost, a professional after all.

Ever true to himself, he disclosed one last bit of wisdom before closing the door. He told me this:

"It's fitting to take pleasure in your old memories Maddy, but they fade for a reason. Don't waste your time trying to recapture every detail of what you perceive to have lost, for while you sap your energy recalling the past, you will miss the now – destroying what chance you have to create a fresh memory – losing it forever."

I called Jane and Paige a short time later under the guise I needed help getting food prepared, before we opened for business tomorrow morning. This wasn't entirely untruthful, as I'd done nothing since pouring through the boxes of my past on Saturday evening.

When they arrived, I was baking muffins, staying busy to keep my nerves intact. My face must have belied the reasons I gave for asking them to come over, as they both demanded to know what was wrong, this instant. I suppose I should have known they wouldn't fall for it. I've never fallen behind in my baking, in all these years. I wasn't certain how or where to start, so I began from the beginning asking them to let me finish everything before the questions began. While I spoke, I continued preparing food focusing on each task while I recited my story, in a factual, distant fashion. I took care to not look while I described the accident, revealing the severity of my losses and divulging the extent of my memory impairment. I knew if I broke my concentration by looking into their faces, I would see their empathy and I wasn't prepared to accept their comfort just yet. I needed to talk through it all again, for me as well as for them, so I too, could fully comprehend the life I'd had and connect it to the present. I knew Jane and Paige would be silent while I spoke although shocked to hear my tale, but they were my friends. They would understand my reasons for keeping my past hidden from them, knowing I could not share something when my own intellectual capacity was lacking.

When I had finished finally forcing my head to lift, my eyes to view their faces, I was surprised to see respect permeating through their smiles. Oh, they had tears in their eyes too, but there wasn't the pity I had remembered from my friends of long ago. It was admiration, like the kind given a war hero. I began to feel warmth spreading up through the soles of my feet, rising slowly until my entire being was consumed, my heart feeling full – beating strong and proud. I began to smile too, as I walked forward ready to accept the comfort I sorely needed, allowing my friends to wrap their arms around me in a circle of love.

Truth is never known

We all lie, even to ourselves.

Grey's Anatomy

Season 2 – Episode 15

RECONNECTIONS

Among the remnants of my boxed memories, was the name, address and phone number for the caretaker in charge of rentals for the beach house my family reserved each year. I knew after watching the slides and video tapes, I would have to go see this place one last time – a completion of the vacation we were taking before fate dealt us its fatal blow. If I was to fully embrace my past, this trip was pertinent. I made the call and arranged the visit, setting up lodging at a hotel nearby. I knew I would be unable to stay at the beach house overnight, for its ghostly memories would be too much for me to endure.

When I approached Paige and Jane, asking them to accompany me to Nags Head, they were eager to do so. Their inclusion was essential, so the reconnection process and final phase of the therapeutic passage Tom had set me on could come to fruition.

Recapturing my past allows me to bridge the gap, fill the void and create the seamless transition necessary, for an uninterrupted flow toward this second life I've carved for myself. I knew I needed to jumpstart my narrative or episodic memory that would allow me to recall personally experienced events, which until recently I had been unable to do. After all, we are our memories. I wanted a greater opportunity for connection, which is why taking this trip back to a place where such happiness and historic records occurred, was key.

I arranged to have a couple of former students I'd mentored in the past cover the operations of the Book and Brew on Saturday, so we could have two days for leisurely travel with one day to reminisce.

When I called the caretaker for the beach house, I wasn't sure the contact information I had would still be accurate. I was pleased when Lily Sanders answered the phone. In fact, she remembered my name right away. When she conveyed her condolences at the onset of our conversation, I was strangely comforted by her voice and also by the knowledge she'd been involved during the years my family had vacationed there – another person who knew them. I talked with her briefly about my life after the accident, concluding with the return of my memory, thus my reasons for going there. She informed me I could have access to the house, during the morning until early after-noon hours on any Sunday, before the arrival of the next tenants. She also expressed her anxiousness in being able to see me again.

The date was set for Sunday, August 7th, 2006 – twenty-five years, two months and four days, after our last scheduled time of arrival.

OUTER BANKS

Paige and Jane were anxious to hear more about our destination, asking me questions incessantly. Shortly after Lily and I had made the arrangements, she sent me some travel brochures, which I shared with them.

The strand of islands spattered along the Outer Banks curves out into the Atlantic Ocean only to meander back again into the comforting embrace of its mainland coast. These islands have survived the onslaught of wind and sea for thousands of years. Many of the towns running along the natural shoreline are rich in history and tradition such as; Kitty Hawk, whose remote location offered privacy, consistent winds, gentle hills perfect for glide launching, and sandy surfaces to protect those landings and was forever carved into aviation history, when Orville and Wilbur Wright selected it as the site for their experiments, in the 1900s.

Further along the coastline there is a 72 mile stretch of undeveloped natural beaches encompassing Bodie Island to the north and Ocracok Island at its southern boundary. Hatteras Island is the centerpiece for the Cape Hatteras National Seashore and its series of seven villages are each distinct, with their own allure and legends.

This area is also known as a 'birdwatchers paradise' where as many as 300 species can be viewed from fall to spring, including great gray swans, blue heron, oystercatchers and falcon.

The five lighthouses, along the Outer Banks, are one of the most popular historical landmarks. The Cape Hatteras Light Station is the tallest brick lighthouse on the American Coast at approximately 198-feet high. During the summers, prior to 2001, visitors could actually climb its 268 cast-iron steps to the lantern room enjoying a wondrous view of the blue-green ocean, the Albemarle Sound, the formation of the Island, as well as sandpipers scampering on the beach.

The town of Nags Head hosts a number of historic cottages located across from the town's most significant landmark, Jockey's Ridge State Park, where the tallest natural sand dune system in the eastern United States is located, offering unparallel views of the town from its heights.

Nags Head has continued to maintain its quaint atmosphere over the years, with family operated businesses and a relaxed pace of life. It is an annual vacation spot for a countless number of families, making it the ideal family beach.

THE BEACH HOUSE

We arrived Saturday late in the afternoon, my pulse quickening with each mile covered, until at last we reached the final right turn, ending at Nags Head. Our hotel, Travelodge Nags Head Beach was actually located in Kill Devil Hills, the next town north.

Driving through town, I tried to recall shops along the way, anything seemingly familiar to me. Much had changed, as may be expected, with the passage of time. I was seeing things for the first time and no recognition flickered anywhere within. Jane was at the wheel and Paige sat quietly looking about, allowing me to absorb the view. We were all tired after the long drive.

"Let's go straight to the hotel, Jane. Tomorrow will be a long day."

"Is there anything you recognize yet?" Paige asked.

"Not really, I barely recount the scenes from the tapes and pictures. I was hoping this visit would help me recall more of it – recapture its charm."

Jane chimes in then – "Don't fret about it Lyn. All in due time is how I think of it. You've faced a lot already. Let's enjoy our time together you never know when the three of us will have the chance to do something like this again."

We lapse once more into silence while traveling toward our lodging – each focusing on the landscape around us, any thoughts unspoken.

After checking into our rooms, we all agree to take a short rest arranging to meet an hour later for dinner. Gathering in the lobby, Paige – ever the organizer, informs us she has already researched the local fare and reserved a table at the Flying Fish Café. The menu featured a variety of dishes its specialty seafood, naturally. I opted for the soup, Thai Coconut Shrimp Bisque with a side salad. Jane, ever adventurous, chose an appetizer of Baked Spinach & Parmesan Pie with Wild Mushrooms & Apple Wood smoked bacon topped with Golden Fried Oysters, along with a Shrimp Caesar salad. Paige settled on a traditional Spinach Salad and a side order of Carolina Crab Cakes. Our window view bore a different feel from that we had seen driving through Nags Head. This area was congested, overrun by commercialism. By the time dinner was complete and we returned to the hotel, it was late evening. We parted ways once more until morning, when the reasons for our visit would begin to play out.

The next day, after a light breakfast, we drove back toward Nags Head following the directions I'd been sent by Lily. This area was decidedly different from Kill Devil Hills. The shops were residential looking, variations of a "cottage" look, with old historic houses along the ocean front blending in with cinder block homes or Spanish-styled souvenir stores. The mixture was chaotic, yet endearing, generating a desire to learn more of its culture and history.

Pulling into the parking area, I view a glimpse of a house and without hesitation I know it's the one I'm here for. I wondered how a place like this could be forgotten under any circumstances. Its beauty rose up from the sand like the castles envisioned by a child on the beach. For a moment, I become wistful, a tear threatening to break free. Quickly, I focus my thoughts on the images of my family, captured in laughter inside this house – shaking away the sadness.

"Lyn, are you coming?" says Paige opening my door for me.

"Yes, of course. I can't wait to show it to you. Let's go."

They allow me to move ahead, dropping back so I can reach the house first. While I stand waiting at the edge of the porch, I look back at them maneuvering their way across the sand. I am blessed to have them as friends. The best part of my life is now about to meld with the best of my past.

I glance up at the house proceeding slowly up the steps. Its beauty has faded some, through wear and tear over the years, but it stands tall in its history. This old house could tell many stories I bet, and as I stand reflecting on this thought, I envision a familiar scene – one of my boys, Ian and Jon, charging past me, clamoring over each other, racing to see who can run the fastest along the wrap-around decks encircling the house. I'm brought back by the voices of Jane and Paige, who are now standing near my side.

I loop my arms into each of theirs and we finish walking up the wide steps to the porch area. Looking toward the ocean I ask them –

"Now girls, have you ever seen anything more beautiful than this?"

Our gazes focus on the expansive beach spread out before us – the sand disappearing amid an aqua-green ocean rippled with white-capped waves in a diminishing pattern, extending backward into the horizon, where beams of light cast upward – touching the edge of the sun risen up from its morning bath. I had hoped to arrive at this time of day – a perfect hour to soak up the memory to its fullest – letting it unfold to breathe, fresh and free.

Our thoughts are interrupted as we hear the wooden screen door creak open. We turn to see an elderly woman approaching us, a warm smile across her face.

"Madelyn, how wonderful it is to see you again" she says extending her hand to touch my arm.

"Hello, Lily," I say as her face immediately rings recognizable. "These are my friends I told you about, Paige and Jane."

"Hello, ladies. It's a pleasure to meet you. I see you've been enjoying the view. What do you think?"

"Utterly breathtaking," says Jane.

"I have to agree," says Paige. "It's beautiful."

"Maddy, there's only a short time to tour the house before the next tenants arrive, so I won't take up any more of your time. I'm sure you have many things you'd like to share with your friends. Meanwhile, I'll excuse myself. I need to follow up on a few minor things. There's a pitcher of fresh sweet tea on the counter in the kitchen for y'all. We'll talk a little later, before you leave."

"Thanks so much, Lily. You're every bit as accommodating now as you were in the past."

As she walks away, I motion to Paige and Jane to follow me into the house. Holding the door for them, I glance across the porch decking at a row of outdoor seating: a couple of Adirondack chairs, the paint worn in spots from continued use, a small table between them; a weathered rocker and; at the end where the porch turns to the left, is a wooden porch swing. For a split second, I see an image of my husband with Lucy on his lap reading her favorite book, *I am Bunny* by Richard Scarry. It was their special time together, while I put the twins down for a nap. When I return my focus to the entry, I see Paige looking back at me, Jane already exploring up ahead.

"Why don't you let us walk through on our own, Lyn. This is your time to reminisce; you can come for us when you need to. By the way, I heard Lily call you Maddy. Was that what people called you before?"

"Yes, they did. When I came to Landrum to begin again, I felt strange about using Maddy, so I introduced myself there as Lyn. It seemed like the right thing at the time."

"I understand perfectly."

That's Paige — always the sensitive one looking out for everyone. I look at her gratefully, thankful to have a friend who knows me so well. I walk across the wooden floors into the large living area, the stone fireplace ready to warm the room when cool evenings approach. The furniture has changed but its contour is still inviting. A coffee table sits ready to play board games or work on a family puzzle. I continue walking toward the bedrooms each with their own private access to the wrap-around decks. As I saunter along room to room, my head plays out different scenes, like turning pages in a photo album. At first the pages appear blank, with only dashes outlining the spot where pictures should be, then miraculously, they are filled in with images solid and real. It reminds me of the sticker books I would buy for the children meant to occupy them, while I prepared dinner.

I find myself standing in the large corner room whose French doors open to a deck facing the ocean. I walk over to the vanity table angled in the corner. I sit down on its stool facing the mirror. I remember sitting here often, my personal effects scattered across its top. My face, reflecting back at me, begins to appear more youthful. I see Neil's image through the glass behind me. I watch him approach and as he does, he leans down to place a kiss at the base of my neck, hitting that sensitive area just above the curve, where your shoulder begins. His kiss is gentle barely grazing my skin and I can feel the softness of his lips followed by a warm tingling radiating through me — even now, as I sit here alone. Closing my eyes, I can smell him, a tiny hint of nutmeg in the air wafting from his skin – natural in its odor, his self-contained cologne.

When I join Paige and Jane, they are in the kitchen enjoying a glass of the tea Lily had left there. I begin to talk about the mealtimes we enjoyed in this room on our vacations.

"You know girls, I can remember my family making sandwiches right here on this very counter. Ian and Jon always wanted to make their own, peanut butter and jelly of course. They always managed to get more of it on themselves then on the bread. I declare, it was a real mess they made, but oh how much fun we had. Neil and I couldn't help but laugh at them, they were quite the pair. What one didn't think of the other certainly did. Lucy on the other hand was quite meticulous, her peanut butter on one slice, jelly on the other, then she would carefully place them together. Those lunches on the beach were the best and you should have seen us making homemade banana splits, the children's faces sticky with a rainbow of colors – my oh my, the talking and laughter we shared."

Jane and Paige are laughing profusely at my description of the scene, when three children burst through the doorway squealing, interrupting us. Their parents, heavily burdened with suitcases, are urging them to please use indoor voices, as they struggle to enter the house. Just then Lily appears in the kitchen,

"I'm afraid the tenants have arrived, Madelyn."

"So we see", I say smiling. "Thanks again for letting us go through the house. I'm ready to go though. Do you mind if we walk along the beach awhile?"

"Of course not, take your time. I'm glad you came; it's been good to see you again. I'd better scoot so I can go over the house rules. You know the routine. Take care Madelyn."

We share a warm hug for a moment before she departs once more, on her way toward providing another family, opportunities for adventures like those we had enjoyed.

Leaving the house, I watch the children still scampering every-where, while Lily talks with the couple. I think of my own family again and I envy the discoveries I know are awaiting them, yet at the same time I feel content in the memories already made.

Heading toward the beach, I make a suggestion to take our shoes off and walk along the shoreline. Jane is all for it, then Paige pipes up suggesting she walk over to one of the beach restaurants nearby to bring back something fruity to sip and maybe a small snack, while Paige secures a few beach chairs. The lure of food and a cool drink appeals more to Jane than a journey through the hot sand, so she urges me to go on without her. Of course, this was Paige's plan all along to allow me more time alone.

This walk is the last thing I had on my list to do for closure. We used to stroll along the shoreline every day, at least once. I knew I needed to step inside those footprints one final time although aware the layer of time has since buried them. Our walks were special – a time of bonding, each sharing moments deemed significant, thus offering a glimpse of our inner souls. Long ago my parents had fore-cast this visit. They knew I would choose this spot to scatter their ashes. I needed the bareness of my feet to touch the water for this would be their final resting place. I reach into the bag I've brought with me and lift out the metal box. I open it up looking down at its contents, then I wade into the water feeling the pull of the tide as it moves back and forth. The wind is blowing at my back so I turn around lifting the box high in the air rotating it slightly so the wind picks them up and carries them out to sea. We've completed our journey here at last – as a family.

Before long, I sit down to rest, the wetness from my feet now covered with sand. I feel its coarseness between my toes.

Looking up, I see sparkles bouncing atop the waves, so bright I am nearly blinded. Soon another memory comes forth.

"Look Mommy! There's diamonds on the water again!"

I lift my head up from the blanket I'm laying on to look at the ocean. Sure enough, just as Lucy's said – the water is filled with diamonds bouncing along the waves, the sun glistening brightly. The effect of sun to water, along with the movement, always takes my breath away – its beauty captivating.

"Count them Lucy."

I watch her as she begins to count, her tiny finger pointing to each one as fast as she can. A couple of minutes later she pouts, "Mommmmmeee, there's too many of them, I can't count that high yet."

"Then pick only one and bring it to me."

She quickly runs back into the water convinced she can grab at least one. She does this every time, without success, but never tires of trying anyway. I watch after her fascinated by her excitement, her never ending belief that someday she will succeed, grasping one tightly to happily place it in my hand, her face beaming proudly. She is such a perfect child, so inquisitive and anxious to learn. Her love of even the simplest things amazes me, her ability to understand when I tease her and the amount of knowledge she has acquired would be far reaching for any other four year old.

She's right I think, there are too many – though at this moment, I feel like she's finally succeeded.

GOING HOME

Coming to terms with my past, has made decisions concerning my retirement fall into place with a greater ease than I first thought possible. The visit Jane, Paige and I made to the beach house was the completion of the circle I needed, to once again become whole. For the first time since the accident, I can see not only where I am headed, but where I've been. My family was mine once again. I could finally grieve over their death, allow myself to feel love – let it wrap its arms around me with its comforts. I could let them go too. It is with this full knowledge and acceptance that I made my plans to go home – back to the place I grew up, had my dreams, fell in love – raised a family.

I am reminded of a book read years back about homing pigeons and their dependability on internal instincts, as well as familiar characteristics along the road, in order to fly home. I was fascinated to learn that in conjunction with internal magnetic "compasses" near their nose and eyes, which may help calculate the Earth's magnetic fields, much of their ability to find their way home, comes from nerves located in their noses. Once these nerves were severed, they became lost.

Perhaps, I think, this is what happened to me. While missing the pieces of my memory, I was unable to find my way home or know exactly where that home might be. Although Landrum became a special place, one I can never forget – it was an important step to take in the ultimate journey back. South Carolina was never fully mine, not like Massachusetts or even its North Carolina sister, the place of the beach house my family so loved. My life was shaped on the Eastern shoreline – the mold was already formed, the fit was always right. This is why I must return.

Everything is in place. I've sold my cupcake recipes to an on-line bakery — imagine that — something so simple will now be available all over the country in record time. As for the bookstore and coffee shop, the former students I asked to cover for us, when we were on our trip, have joined partnership and decided to purchase it. They tell me it was a mainstay in their lives and they hate to see it go – keeping my spirit alive, they claim.

"Hey there Lyn, how goes the packing?"

I turn at the sound of Jane's voice, as she comes through the door.

"Good afternoon Jane. Everything is close to being done, I think. Are you and Ed getting ready to take off on your trip out West?"

"Ed's outside waiting for me. I wanted to make sure you were all set before we took off or see if you needed any last minute help. I also wanted to make sure you had our numbers handy, so you know how to get in touch with us."

"I've got them, right here, yours and Paige's too", I say as I lift my address book sitting near me on the counter. "You have a good time. Don't worry about me, I'm fine – only a bit of a headache, but I'm sure that's because I need to eat something. You get going now and enjoy yourselves you've got a long drive ahead of you."

She gives me one last hug and waves back at me, as she heads out the door. I think back on the time I first met her, when I was surrounded by boxes like now – only then I was unpacking getting ready to open the business up. Such a long time ago, my how far we've come together. Instead of her motorcycle, she's sporting a huge motor home for transportation these days – a sign of the aging process I suppose or stiffened bones. She rode it far into her early 60s though before she'd give it up. I find myself smiling at the remembrance – Jane always made me feel good – alive.

I wince at a sharp pain that shoots through my head reminding myself I must take a break, get something to eat. I begin to walk toward the refrigerator, when a hot numbness enters my face then cascades along my right arm. I reach for the phone on the counter with my left hand, as the feeling continues its downward momentum, traveling down my side causing my leg to break way beneath me, void of its ability to fulfill its function of support. Before I lose consciousness, I see the lights blurring overhead, reminiscent of a falling star streaking across the blackened sky far above the sandy beach, as I fall in slow motion toward the floor.

THE WRITER

I slowly close my laptop while reflecting on the ending. I've reached the conclusion of my journey into a life I feel so close to – it could have been mine. There is numbness on the tips of my fingers, shallowness in my breathing, and stillness throughout my body's frame as I sit motionless. The story is over – finished. I should feel relief. Instead, I feel lost, like a broken compass unable to detect direction.

I look around the room, seeing its furnishings with a freshened eye. This spot has been my sanctuary. I begin to run my fingers lightly over the surface of the mahogany desktop. I marvel at its smoothness, the depth of its rich burgundy grains coursing through the wood. My gaze follows the lines lifting upward to a silver framed family picture, smiles looking back at me lovingly – my own image as well, yet I can't recall when or where it was taken. It is at that moment, I realize how much I've missed, not only from this latest venture of mine, but for years now. While I've been pursuing my own self-fulfillment, I allowed time to rob me of those small pleasures children slip in as blessings every day.

I stand up to walk toward the window looking out over the gardens. The sun is glistening through the woods filled with aging White Oak trees towering high above my view. The light weaves itself among the leaves like ribbons intertwined with darkness. There are spots of light that manage to break through despite the density, like a flame of fire deep within a pyramid of logs refusing to be denied its right to glow. A soft breeze causes the pansies below – brilliant yellows, purples, pinks and reds – to dance with the light, a color wheel of ballerinas pirouetting, arms swaying gently in time to a musical concerto orchestrated by Carolina wrens, whose whistled notes seem to say *tea-kettle, tea-kettle.*

I am here alone. My family has gone somewhere, perhaps a movie. I've been consumed, refusing their offers of inclusion so often they no longer bother to ask. Although they've seen a change in me this past year, I have remained aloof – not willing to share myself with anyone but her. Through the story, she revealed to me my selfishness exposing a stunted compassion, a self-gratifying individual blinded to the gifts I'd been afforded – the focus not on me, but on those who've stood by me, supported me all along, asking little in return. I aver to change course hoping there's still time.

While I await their return, I begin browsing through magazines piled up on the counter. I come across an article describing the powers of the mind, a subject of interest since the morning I awoke, inspired by my dream. As I continue to read, I am intrigued by the subjects studied and the concepts introduced. Turning the page, it is the last situation described that causes my heart to quiver – a chill to travel along my spine. I place a call to Collingswood Hills, the location listed in the study, then rush upstairs to pack an overnight bag. Suddenly, I stop before I head out the door, reminding myself I am acting upon my own needs, placing myself first, yet again. My struggle is short lived and I quickly scribble a note letting them know I am gone. I promise to return soon, assuring them things have changed, all the while wondering if I have sealed my fate, having stretched their forgiveness to the breaking point. I cannot bear to think of losing them, yet I'm guided by a force more powerful, knowing I am risking it all, to find the answer.

COLLINSWOOD HILLS

"I'm afraid she isn't going to offer you much in the way of company, at least not in the traditional sense."

"That's fine … um, what did you say your name was? By the way, I'm Dana Carroll but please, call me Dana."

"Hello, Dana. I'm Abigail Martin, a Psychiatric Physicians Assistant. Madelyn is under my care here and has been for many years. We've a long history together. I understand you read an article describing a study done with Madelyn as one of the subjects, is that correct?"

"Yes, it was very intriguing and I was hoping I could meet with her, but first I was wondering if you could give me some background on her case."

"Well, I'm afraid some of her information is privileged however I can elaborate a bit on the subject matter covered through the study or some generic information, if that would help."

"What ever you can say would be appreciated."

"All right then. Why don't I start by filling you in on how Madelyn came to live here and what her condition remains to be? As the article said, she suffers from a condition referred to as Post-Coma Unresponsiveness or PCU, which is different from a typical Coma.

Rather than existing in a deep sleep, PCU patients appear to sleep and wake normally, but do not show signs they are aware of their surroundings or the people they encounter. They are not brain dead. However, their ability for responsiveness is restricted."

"Do they know what is happening around them, Abigail?"

"It's unlikely they do, but we can never be certain. There are many medical mysteries, this only one of them. Sometimes a person will moan or show facial responses, which could be attributed to reflex actions rather than an actual awareness. Madelyn has shown some of these signs and for a period she showed signs of entering another stage described as a minimally responsive state, or MRS where she actually said a couple of words, her eyes at times clearing as though she could recognize the people around her, but these periods were short lived.

In the beginning, her parents tried to care for her at home a trying situation not often encouraged. However, she was all they had and they felt it their duty to try and reach her. They'd hoped she would recognize the familiar surroundings and eventually awake fully. They had parties inviting old friends and made trips to places they felt sure she would recall – all to attempt stimulation of her mind. They were already elderly though, when the accident happened and caring for Madelyn began to take its toll on their health. When Paul had his first heart attack, they had to face facts and let her go. It was heartbreaking for them, but in the end they made arrangements to move her back to our facility. Oddly, Madelyn seemed happier then she'd been in a long time making her parents decision easier for them to accept.

Her parents were consistent visitors until they passed but never gave up hope she would recover, reading to her every day to keep her current with the world, its historical changes especially. They celebrated birthdays and holidays with cupcakes – a favorite of hers as a child. She also had visits from her psychologist, who grew fond of Madelyn during her initial recovery phase. Her condition haunted him and he couldn't let go of his efforts to get through to her. When her parents passed on, he continued in their place filling in a history she no longer remembered while educating her on various life experiences or other situations he thought she would be interested in."

"Would it be possible to talk with him?"

"No, Dana. I'm sorry to say, Tom passed away recently. I'm not sure if Madelyn misses his visits or not but I told her anyway. I've always felt something still existed there though I have no proof. I guess I'm…."

"Excuse me, Abigail. Did you say his name was Tom?"

"Yes, I did. Why?"

"It's only that … well…. I'm sure it's a coincidence but when I read about Madelyn, I thought something seemed familiar about her. It struck a cord that resonated inside me and now you mention the name Tom, but – you say she's never awoken, right?"

"That's right. What are you saying?"

"I don't know, just speculating I suppose. Do you think I could see Madelyn for a moment?"

"Certainly, I can't see any harm in it. She only has me now. Maybe she'd like to hear a new voice. Don't expect too much, Dana. She's very fragile as you can imagine and she's suffered a stroke recently."

As I enter her room, I notice a number of pictures on the ceiling above her bed. For the second time, I am filled with certainty – a nervous flutter in my heart as I approach. I lean down turning my face upward in the same direction as hers for a better view. There is one of an older couple – maybe her parents; another of three young women; a house on the shore; and in the center a picture of a family

– her family I expect – a man, a healthy younger Madelyn, a blond-haired girl and two younger boys – one dark, the other blond. I know it's impossible, yet I wonder. I lift my head turning it back to the bed. I am inches away from her face. It happens so fast, I'm not sure my eyes registered it at all or if my desire for an answer has played tricks in my mind.

There was a glimmer of light that shone in her eyes, a diamond sparklingly faintly within and she smiled as though she knew me, then darkness cast its shadow once more.

UNCONSCIOUSNESS HYPOTHESIS

When I left Madelyn's room, I asked Abigail if I could read some of the other research that the physicians at Collinswood had performed. I found that while many theories exist on the level of consciousness a person may experience when falling into a comatose state, none can positively dispute, whether in a deep sleep or fully aware, if a person can think logically or dream. It's been said that activities in your repetitious dreams can be subconsciously steered in a direction or outcome more favorable.

I read of a case study led by Dr. Adrian Owen, a neuroscientist at the University of Cambridge and colleagues where a woman judged to be in a persistent vegetative state was given a type of exam where blood flow to active parts of the brain could be detected. When instructed to imagine the rooms of her home, those areas of the brain involved in navigating space and recognition of places showed gradual increase.

There are religions believing the soul is the source of consciousness that can survive our death, while others believe consciousness is life itself. It does not depend on language, for persons unable to converse still equate consciousness. Neither can self-awareness be a determining factor as many of us lose ourselves in books, exercise or music.

It is conceivable that a person must choose the kinds of accessible information we contain in our thoughts, given the amount of data coming at us from every direction. The brain would short circuit, if expected to decipher everything transported its way. As a result, we compartmentalize or summarize events most important in understanding our situations. Hence, manipulation of ones thoughts is possible to perform.

Rather than postulate on a person's value of life, it may behoove us to leave that decision to them, even if our awareness of their choice may be unknown. In treating patients unable to verbalize or otherwise signal their needs, some feel an atmosphere of stimulation should be provided, instead of one filled with silence or lack of hope.

If an unconscious mind can imagine, then can it not also continue to dream of places it's been or places it wishes to go? And even complete a life not yet finished?

Perhaps a person's subconscious can also possess the capability of opening internal corridors, some reachable by those outside, whose desires mirror their own.

We can all become trapped inside ourselves – some within the confinement of our bodies unable to physically move yet choosing to imagine; others within restricted minds unable to think beyond our own thoughts wasting time sitting idle.

THE SUMMIT

When the stranger departs, I return to my place of comfort feeling satisfied that at last people will know them. I observe Abigail as she enters my room accompanied by another aide I've not yet met. Together they position my body into the chair. Abigail takes care to place my legs and arms in a way that will provide me some relief, as by now she knows how weary they become from their constant state of uselessness. She wheels me in front of the window so I can view the water.

I watch mesmerized as the water moves in and out and I ponder its mysteries, wondering if it chooses who is allowed to ride the wave that reaches its shore. How many only get halfway before going under, although they have maneuvered it well? Is it a journey of chance that determines the outcome or a random selection by a power we cannot control? Can we change our fate, or that of someone else? Would we – if we could?

As I linger on the edge of sleep, I begin to dream of a final adventure, the wave that lifts me up bringing me closer to the shore. In the distance, I see them – waiting for me, anxiously waving me in. I stretch my arms out wide. They are filled with an energy I have not felt in some time. I feel them push apart the water, opening up a path before me. As I thrust forward with a strength borne of desire, pure and filled with longing, I take in a breath and close my eyes while I ride the wave home.

EPILOGUE

Within each of us, there lies a story. Some are filled with song while others barely emit an audible murmur – some are vivid shining brightly on the world, while others hover in shadows buried deep within.

None the less, we are given gifts – each and every one of us. They lay the foundation for the stories we create, the music we wish to sing, and the lives we long to lead. How soon or how late they are discovered depends upon us. We are blessed with free will, the power to choose our ending, good or bad.

Through those who are filled with pain and sadness, hope reigns triumphant, for nothing is ever lost completely. It may just take awhile to find. It's there for you, awaiting discovery – perhaps around the corner or possibly in your dreams.

"There will come a time when you believe everything is finished.

That will be the beginning."

Louis L'Amour

Acknowledgements

This book has been an adventure for me providing yet another opportunity to learn more about myself. What I also discovered though was a group of supporters I never knew I had in coworkers, business owners, and acquaintances a person encounters day-to-day; some of who I may never run across again. I feel compelled to mention Carole and Jan, who read my first writings and offered encouragement when I needed it the most. My coffee house friends Erin, Paige and the 'Sarahs', who never failed to ask me how the book was coming along inspiring me each day to keep going. Some of the stories and experiences I've had with friends have been passed on in these pages and I want to thank them for allowing me to share these good times with my readers. Of course, there is always my family and everyone did their part in offering me the assurances I needed to finish, especially my husband, Carlos and daughter-in-law, Cheryl Anne. They both listened graciously while I talked aloud my thoughts keeping me grounded and focused on the right path. Special recognitions go to my grandchildren – Mallory, Cassidy and Tanner – who with a simple smile could light up anyone's world and make them do extraordinary things.

AFTERWORD

When the idea for this book first came to me, I began to draw upon my own experiences and knowledge as every good writer knows he or she should do. Having worked at least a decade in the medical field afforded me the opportunity to view various illnesses, procedures and practices that occur in a hospital setting. However, I did draw on outside information via the internet that allowed me to further educate myself in areas involving brain injury and treatment. I consulted these resources: bio-medical.com, *Coma: A State of Profound Unconsciousness* by Robert J. Doman, M.D.; WebMD. com/a-to-z-guides; healthatoz.com and a July 15, 2008 archived publication by the Commonwealth of Australia 2005 at http://nla.gov. au/nla.arc-86845.

Actual locations and tourist attractions mentioned in this fictional writing are places I have visited many times that hold a special place in my heart. I consulted their web pages to bring forth information to share with others including Madelyn and her friends. Those resources include: www.outerbanks.org; www.nps.gov Cape Hatteras National Seashore; www.landrumchamber.com; www.chimneyrockpark. com and www.biltmore.com.

The song lyrics used from, *You are my sunshine* are credited to former Governor Charles Mitchell and Jimmie Davis – 1937.

Quote – madeleinemoments.com, trans. By C.K. Scott Moncrief and Terence Kilmartin. Proust, Marcel. *Remembrance of Things Past.* New York: Vintage Books (Random House) I, II & III. 1982

Lastly, I consulted my personal Bible and oaks.nvg.org/cayce5. html on the subject of dreams.

I hope you are inspired by these sources as much as I was.